DEAD GUN

Ray Hogan

Chivers Press   •   G.K. Hall & Co.
Bath, England   Waterville, Maine USA

This Large Print edition is published by Chivers Press, England, and by G.K. Hall & Co., USA.

Published in 2001 in the U.K. by arrangement with the author c/o Golden West Literary Agency.

Published in 2001 in the U.S. by arrangement with Golden West Literary Agency.

U.K. Hardcover ISBN 0-7540-4574-9 (Chivers Large Print)
U.K. Softcover ISBN 0-7540-4575-7 (Camden Large Print)
U.S. Softcover ISBN 0-7838-9473-2 (Nightingale Series Edition)

The text of this Large Print edition is unabridged.
Other aspects of the book may vary from the original edition.

Set in 16 pt. New Times Roman.

Printed in Great Britain on acid-free paper.

British Library Cataloguing in Publication Data available

Library of Congress Cataloging-in-Publication Data

    Hogan, Ray, 1908–
      Dead gun / Ray Hogan.
        p. cm.
      ISBN 0-7838-9473-2 (lg. print : sc : alk. paper)
      1. Large type books.   I. Title.
      PS3558.O3473 D388 2001
      813'.54—dc21   2001024204

DEAD GUN

CHAPTER ONE

When the muffled cry for help reached Parsonville's town marshal, Jake Royce, he lunged to his feet and hurriedly crossed to the door. It was late in the day and he had been sitting at his desk in the small, stuffy office searching through a stack of outlaw wanted posters for a certain face.

Taut, he reached the exit and, stepping out onto the landing, glanced about. The street was quiet and, in deference to the intense heat, entirely deserted, except for two women in front of Tom Bell's Hardware Store studying the items displayed in the window, and the slight figure of Aaron Dunn, the town's mayor as well as its feed and seed merchant, leaning in the entrance to his establishment.

'Over here—help!'

Royce spun, threw his glance to the squat structure housing the general store, some fifty yards or so on down the street. Max Kastman, the owner, was coming through the doorway, reeling badly, his face streaked with blood.

Drawing his pistol, Royce stepped off the stoop and headed for the man at a fast run. Back up the way he saw Dunn, attracted by Kastman's exhausted cry, also break into a run for the store.

Royce reached the sprawling structure,

1

bounded up the three steps, and caught the merchant under the arms just as he began to fall.

'Robbers!' Kastman gasped through crushed lips. 'Beat me—took my money—all of it!'

Holstering his weapon, Royce lowered the man to a sitting position and, supporting him with an arm, looked closely at Kastman's battered face. The man had been brutally pistol-whipped.

'Where are they now, Max?' the lawman asked, looking about as Dunn, accompanied by two citizens who had joined him on the way, came up onto the store's wide landing. 'You see where they went?'

'For—for their horses,' Kastman replied haltingly. 'I hear them say—to hurry—to go to their horses. They left them—at the side—of Benson's—in the brush.'

Benson's—the livery stable. It stood opposite, at the far end of the street. Shifting his eyes quickly to that point, Royce could see two horses standing slack-hipped in the ragged growth a bit north of the peak-roofed building.

'How many of them, Max?' Dunn asked.

'Two. They make me think they were customers, looking around and—and asking prices. And then they—they took their pistols—beat me—knock me down. They think I am—dead—but I hear them talk.'

Jake, surrendering his place at Kastman's side to Dunn, drew himself stiffly erect. The

2

outlaws were still in the settlement, somewhere, and were at that moment endeavoring to get to their horses. The lawman gave brief wonder as to why they would leave their mounts at one end of the town and rob a store at the other. He decided they had probably worked their way along the empty street until they found the most promising prospect, which proved to be Kastman's, and then struck.

'They've not gone yet,' Royce heard Dunn say. 'Max says their horses are down near Benson's—'

'I heard,' the lawman cut in coolly. He and Aaron Dunn were not on the best of terms, since Dunn, in his capacity of mayor, had found much fault on numerous occasions with the way Royce conducted his office.

They had a basic difference of opinion when it came to the handling of outlaws. Dunn took the position that a lawbreaker, whatever his crime, was entitled to be treated with consideration. Jake Royce, of the old school, trained in the world of hard-case, violent men, saw it only one way: an outlaw was an outlaw and deserved nothing except punishment for the crime he had committed.

Royce granted no more than that—and such was the bone of contention between them; it had become steadily more pronounced and serious when the lawman, never relenting in what he considered his duty, continued to

3

bring in prisoners slung across their saddles.

At first, when Royce had pinned on the Parsonville star of town marshal, it had been a matter of great pride to the people of the settlement to have a man of Jake Royce's caliber looking out for them. Being only a few miles from one of the major cattle trails, the town was frequented regularly by drovers as well as the riffraff who customarily derive profit from the men who move the herds.

Thus crime, periodically, was high in Parsonville, and a lawman with a fast, deadly gun was looked upon as an asset. Jake Royce's reputation and ability proved that point, but as the years wore on, whispered accusations were to be heard; he had become too quick with his gun, too prone to shoot—he had evolved into a killer marshal. If the town, some declared, were to survive, it could no longer afford to keep him on the job.

There was nothing new in the concept. It was occurring throughout the frontier—the natural result of growth, of a town getting larger and consequently more dependent on outside patronage if its existence was to continue.

Neither Dunn nor any other member of the town's council had ever openly brought the matter up to Royce, but the mayor did hint now and then that he should think more along the lines of bringing arrested miscreants in for trial by jury rather than for the attentions of

Ira Peabody, the local undertaker.

'They're somewheres along the street,' Dunn said. 'They got to get to their horses so's they can line out of here—'

Royce nodded. His glance was probing along the buildings, seeking a sign of the two men hiding in a doorway, an inset, or in one of the several passageways that lay between some of the structures.

'I can holler for help, get some men together and try surrounding the—'

Royce shook his head before the mayor could complete the suggestion. 'No time for that . . . I'll take care of it. They'll never get to those horses,' he added.

Dunn, helping Kastman, who by then had recovered full senses, to his feet, frowned. 'I'd as soon you took them alive, Marshal.'

'It's up to them,' Royce snapped. 'They'll get their chance to quit, throw down their iron, and come peaceable. If they don't want it that way—'

The lawman didn't complete the sentence. Shoulders set, he descended the steps of the store landing and moved off through the ankle-deep dust of the street in the direction of Benson's stable and the horses waiting in the brush nearby.

He kept to the center of the wide lane, knowing that while he perhaps made a good target of himself, he was also in a better position to see any movement on either side as

5

he strode purposefully along.

Royce was a tall man, lean, darkened by the sun, and with perpetually narrowed gray eyes. The star pinned to the pocket of his checked shirt glinted sharply in the slanting sunlight, and his wide-brimmed hat, stained by sweat and dust, rode well forward on his head, providing shade for his restless glance.

His bleached cord pants were tucked into boots that bore many scars, and the worn-handled forty-five that he carried in a darkly oiled holster rode high and well forward on his right thigh.

That he was a man of single, intense mind, one with little patience for anyone at variance with his convictions, was evident in the hard set of his jaw and the firm, straight line of his mouth. Sweat was beading his forehead, but of that he seemed unaware; he simply strode relentlessly on in the breathless hush that gripped the town, like a great cat stalking its prey and refusing to be distracted.

'Marshal!' The voice was a hoarse whisper coming from the trash-and weed-filled corridor lying between Wilson's Saddle and Harness Shop and the widow Davis's Ladies & Children's Clothing Store. 'Marshal!'

Royce slowed his step slightly, let his stony gaze drift to the passageway. It was old Abe Goodson, one of the swampers at Charlie Brock's saloon.

'Yeh?'

'I seen them! I seen them two you're looking for!' Goodson replied in a quick rush of words. 'They was legging it for them horses over by the stable.'

'Where'd you see them?'

'They ducked into that old empty building across from there—from the stable.'

'When?'

'Not more'n a couple of minutes ago. I seen them come up alongside and stop and look up the street. They seen you coming and real quick run and got inside. Was two of them.'

Royce nodded, said, 'Obliged,' and continued, his attention now fixed on the building Goodson had indicated. He doubted the old man had witnessed the incident at the general store, but the pair he'd seen undoubtedly were the outlaws who had clubbed Kastman and taken his money.

Royce began to veer to the west side of the street, angling slightly toward the structure Abe Goodson had pointed out. It was a low, flat-roofed building that once had been a restaurant with the owner's living quarters in the rear. The enterprise had failed and the place had been boarded up, but as time passed drifters had torn off the barricade that blocked the doorway and used the building for sleeping on cold nights.

Royce had been aware of this, but he could see no great harm in it, recalling, perhaps, the early days when, fresh from Ohio, he did a

7

great deal of knocking about the country, often broke and needing shelter from inclement weather. His one restriction was that no fires were to be built, and anyone not adhering to that edict was ordered to move on. To date the rule had not been broken.

Royce gained the front of the building, paused. He could hear nothing but the dry clack of insects in the weeds growing along the side of the structure, but there was no doubt in his mind that the outlaws were inside. Drawing his pistol, he eased silently up to the open door and halted just outside. Again he listened.

A thread of satisfaction coursed through him. Somewhere within the old restaurant someone had moved. The sound of cloth scraping against the rough surface of wood had reached him clearly.

The sound, it seemed to him, had arisen deep inside the building and not from the fairly large front room that had served as the dining area. The pair were probably hiding in one of the smaller chambers that made up the living quarters. There was no escaping from any of those, the lawman knew. The boards that had been nailed across the windows and the rear door were still securely in place.

Abruptly Royce stepped through the doorway and jerked to one side. The move had raised no challenge, thus proving his belief that the outlaws were somewhere in the rear. Hunched low in the shadows of a back corner of the room, he faced the arched opening that led to the adjoining quarters.

'You two—I've got you covered!' he called. 'Ain't no way out of here other'n the front door—and you won't ever get by me. Smart thing to do is throw down your guns and come out with your hands up.'

There was no response, and the only sounds were the clicking of the insects in the weeds and the distant barking of a dog. The lawman shifted his position, pressing himself closer to the wall in which the archway had been cut, thereby gaining a point where he would not be immediately seen by the outlaws when—and if—they chose to shoot their way out.

'You hear me? Come out now or—'

Two bent figures lurched suddenly through the archway. Pistols in hand, they pivoted to line the weapons on Jake Royce. The lawman reacted instinctively, fired instantly. The reports of his weapon blended with those of the outlaws.

Both men staggered, began to fall as Jake's bullets drove into them. The taller of the pair brought up his pistol for another try at the lawman. Again Royce triggered his forty-five-twice. The outlaws rocked once more from the impact of heavy bullets smashing into them. Then, with the room filled with swirling smoke and the sharp smell of burnt gunpowder, both went down to sprawl full length on the dusty floor.

9

CHAPTER TWO

Royce slowly drew himself upright in the pungent haze. Features grim, he deliberately, almost absently, raised his pistol, thumbed open the loading gate. Rodding out the spent cartridges, he inserted fresh shells into the weapon's cylinder.

Outside in the street there was the hurried pound of running feet as those hearing the gunshots and now deeming it safe to approach rushed to investigate. The doorway darkened as the first to arrive entered. It was Aaron Dunn. Close on his heels were Tom Bell and the battered Max Kastman, the blood on his face and head now dried to a dark crust. There were others—ordinary citizens as well as merchants, but they hung back, remained clustered around the front of the onetime cafe.

Dunn, his beet-red skin darker than usual, cast an angry glance at Jake Royce, who was standing mute against a wall, and dropped to a crouch beside the nearest of the outlaws, lying face down on the floor. Taking the body by a shoulder, he rolled it over. The slouch hat came off, and a wealth of honey-colored hair spilled out about the head.

'My God!' Kastman breathed hoarsely. 'It's Nellie Yarbro!'

'Nellie Archer—she's married now,' Dunn

corrected, and turned the second outlaw onto his back so that the face, young, clean-shaven, narrow, might be seen. 'That there's her husband—Luke.'

Dunn swung his attention to Royce as word of the outlaws' identity and their fate rippled through the crowd outside.

'Can see what I said done no damn good. You went right ahead, killed—'

The tall lawman, eyes all but shut, was staring down at the dead girl's dust-smudged features while something akin to shock passed through him. He was not well acquainted with Nellie and knew but little of the Yarbro family—a widow woman with three sons and a daughter who lived on a small ranch a dozen miles or so southwest of town. The Yarbros had all kept pretty much to themselves, seldom being seen in Parsonville and preferring to do their buying in Evanston, a settlement on to the north of them. Archer, the girl's husband, was a stranger.

'You hear what I said, Royce?' Dunn pressed, his tone still angry.

'Had no choice,' the lawman replied. 'Hate it, but there was nothing else I could do.'

'Always seems to be your story,' Dunn snapped.

Royce shrugged, dropped his pistol back into the holster. 'They came out shooting. You figure I ought to just stand there, do nothing?'

'I've heard that before, too,' the mayor said

icily as he glanced down at Nellie Archer: 'Going to be all the worse for us—you killing a woman. Can't figure why the hell you couldn't've held off and—'

'How was I to know one of them was a woman? She's dressed up like a man—was acting like one.' The lawman paused, turned to Kastman. 'You took her for a man, didn't you, Max?'

The merchant shook his head. 'Didn't see much so I can't say. All happened so fast, after they jumped me—'

'You said they looked around, acted like regular customers aiming to buy something. Appears to me you must've got a good look at them both.'

Kastman's shoulders lifted, fell. 'No, never did get no good look—they kept turning away from me.'

'So you figured her for a man—'

The merchant's thin shoulders stirred again. 'Well, yes, guess I did.'

'Which don't mean nothing,' Dunn stated promptly. 'We've got a dead woman on our hands, shot down by our town marshal—and that ain't going to set a'tall with folks. Goes double for you, Royce—considering your reputation.' He paused as a squat, white-haired man carrying a small satchel bustled through the crowd jamming the doorway and entered the room.

'Ain't no call for you wasting time, Doc,' the

12

mayor continued. 'They're both dead.'

Henry Gossage, the physician, ignored Dunn's words and knelt beside the two bodies. 'Being the coroner, I expect it's my duty,' he murmured, and then frowning, said, 'That's the Yarbro girl. Who's the man?'

'Her husband. Name's Luke Archer.'

'Outlaws, eh? What'd they do?'

'Held up my store, beat me,' Kastman answered.

Gossage turned to the merchant, wagged his head. 'Looks like you need me a lot more than they do,' he said, and pointing a finger at one of the men standing in the doorway, added: 'Go get Ira Peabody. These two are a job for the undertaker now . . . Max, follow mc over to my officc. Want to have a good look at you.'

Dunn laid a restraining hand on the physician's shoulder as he drew himself upright. 'We've got to hold a council meeting. I'll be needing Max so's he can vote. You, too, Doc.'

Gossage frowned, drawing both his white brows together. 'A meeting? What for?'

'Got to decide what we're going to do about the marshal. Things've reached the point where we can't go along with his ways any further.'

The physician rubbed at his chin and then motioned at Kastman to precede him through the doorway. 'Yes, it seems we do have us a problem. But I best look Max over first in case he's been seriously hurt. Go ahead, call your meeting, Aaron, but make it for an hour from now.'

Gossage started to move on, hesitated, pointed a finger at Royce. 'He going to be there so's he can tell his side of it?'

Dunn said, 'Won't be no need. We know all the facts. He said these two came out shooting at him—and that the girl looked like a man to him.'

'Her being a woman shouldn't cut any hay. She is dressed like a man, and female outlaws can kill you just as dead as male ones.'

Dunn swore. 'That ain't the point, Doc! No doubt it was just the way the marshal says—it's what's happened in the past—all the killings and such—that we've got to think about. This here shooting's just brought it all to a head.'

Gossage gave that a moment's thought. 'Yes, I guess you're right,' he said, and glanced at Jake, who was quietly taking it all in. 'You're not saying much, Marshal.'

The lawman smiled tightly. 'Not much use. Seems everybody's got their minds made up about me.'

'You've got to admit your record ain't so good!' Dunn declared. 'Was four killings you did last year bringing in prisoners—those two cowhands that'd been accused of rustling and—'

'They decided they'd rather shoot it out

14

with me than come back here and get hung,' Royce cut in coolly.

'And that stagecoach robber. Witnesses say you shot him down without a reason.'

'Not the way of it,' Royce said, hanging tight to his temper. 'He reached into his coat. I figured he was going for a belly gun.'

'Was he?'

Royce shook his head. 'Nope. Sure didn't find one on him.'

'You see!' Dunn said triumphantly. 'You don't ever wait to be sure about anything—you just go ahead, shoot, and then do your looking.'

'Seems to me the marshal couldn't do much else at a time like that,' Tom Bell said, breaking his silence. 'Was no way in the world he could tell if that man had a hideaway gun or not.'

'And he'd be a damned fool to wait and find out,' Gossage said dryly, starting toward the door. 'He'd be dead then, and knowing for sure wouldn't do him any good. When you're ready to hold the meeting give me a holler and I'll come.'

'I'll be expecting you, too, Max,' Dunn said, nodding. 'I want a full council vote on this.'

The mayor watched the two men push their way through the crowd in the doorway and disappear into the street, and then he brought his attention back to Royce.

'Want you to understand one thing,

15

Marshal,' he said, 'there's nothing personal in this. It's just that my job's to look out for the town's best interests and the way you've been handling your job the last couple of years, well, it just ain't doing us no good.'

'You've got a clean, safe, town, Mister Mayor,' Royce said with a hard smile. Not many this close to the cattle trails can say that.'

'Maybe not, but we're all hurting for business. Some of us are going broke, in fact, and that's all come about thanks to the reputation you've built for yourself as a fast gun—too fast, if you want the gospel truth.

'You've got the cowhands and drovers—and pilgrims, too—scared to come around. The word is that if they get the least bit out of line, like drinking a mite too much or celebrating a little wild, or even getting into a scrap, they're liable to end up in the graveyard. Folks are saying that you ain't a man no more—that you're a gun.'

'What folks think's never bothered me much,' Royce replied. 'And when anybody gets out of hand, it's my job to settle them down—with whatever force is necessary.'

'That so? Then what about that cowhand that you shot early this year? I'll admit you didn't kill him, but he ended up in mighty bad shape—and all he was doing at that shindig was having some fun.'

'All he was doing,' Royce echoed in a scornful tone, 'was unloading his gun at the feet of that drummer from Chicago and making him dance a jig when he saw him shining up to the Hoover girl.'

'There was nothing wrong with that—'

'Maybe you don't think so, Mayor, but a dance is no place for a lot of reckless gunplay.'

'Still no reason for your shooting him.'

'Was a reason—a good one. When I called his hand, told him to throw down his gun, he turned it on me. Any man does that he best figure on me coming right back at him.'

'Oh, he wasn't aiming to shoot you,' Dunn said, stubbornly. 'Was only figuring to show off in front of them girls.'

'Maybe,' Royce said, shrugging and moving for the door. 'I reckon it's only him that knows for sure. I didn't, and I done what I had to . . . Now, when you and the town council gets your minds made up about me, I'll be in my office, waiting to hear.'

'Expect you know already what the decision'll be,' Dunn said as Ira Peabody, followed by his son, entered the room with stretchers and blankets for the dead outlaws.

Jake Royce, hesitating at the door, glanced back. 'All I know for certain about it is that I done my job the best I could,' he said, and continued on his way.

CHAPTER THREE

As Jake Royce stepped out into the street the crowd gathered around and, on the landing fronting the abandoned building, hurriedly gave way. A hard grin cracked the lawman's mouth. Once they had looked upon him as their friend—protector, actually. Now they were treating him as if he had plague.

Royce said nothing, however, but moved off down the board sidewalk in the direction of the structure where he maintained a combination of office, jail, and living quarters.

Here and there along the way he caught sight of faces in windows peering out at him vacantly while others, standing in the doorway of their establishments or at the mouth of one of the several passageways between the buildings along the street, eyed him equally emotionlessly. Again a bitter grin broke his stolid visage, and the thought came to him: *this is like the army—like being drummed out of the service in disgrace before friends and enemies both.*

But I'm not out yet, not until they tell me, he thought as he reached his office. Halting there, hand resting on the butt of his pistol, he pivoted slowly. Then, brushing back the hat worn tipped forward over his slotted eyes, he let his glance sweep along the street.

18

Five years—that's what he'd given Parsonville. Five years of damn good lawing—and the facts were there to prove it. His gaze paused on Tom Bell's Hardware Store. He had stopped a robbery in progress there one cold winter night. Brock's Saloon—how many ruckuses had he put a halt to there? The Valley Hotel: there'd been a shooting—a businessman from nearby Evanston who had walked in on his wife in bed with another man.

The fellow had killed both of them. Then Royce arrived, after being summoned by the hotel's clerk, but he came moments too late to halt the murders. The man took it in mind to shoot it out with the lawman and had come off second best. Later it was thought he had intentionally turned on Royce, courting what he apparently knew was certain death.

Davis's Ladies & Children Shop . . . It had been he who spotted the fire inside the store late one cold night when he was making his rounds, and he set up the alarm that prevented what would have been a tragic loss to the elderly widow. And Hans Schulte's Blue Mountain Bank and the holdup that failed—thanks to him. The Trail Driver Restaurant; Wilson's Saddlery & Harness Shop; Benson's Livery Stable; Kastman's; the Home Cafe, owned and operated by a woman friend of his, Della Harper—there was hardly a place in the settlement for which he had not been called upon, in one way or another, to be of service.

19

But he reckoned Aaron Dunn and the council—and most of the town, evidently—were not remembering that. He'd simply worn out his usefulness since his way of upholding the law was no longer acceptable. It was sad—and it was wrong. It would be much better if the bleeding hearts would bleat a little less for the outlaws and a bit more for the victims.

Coming back around, Jake Royce stepped up into his office, which was breathless with trapped heat at that time of day, and hanging his hat on a nail driven into the wall for such purpose, he crossed the room and sat down at his desk.

Except for the break in his life's routine and the loss of familiar faces, he wouldn't mind moving on too much. He'd have no trouble finding a job; there were countless towns looking for lawmen who could keep the peace—and he damn sure had proven that he could do that.

And maybe the next town he took over would appreciate his ways and methods and not be pestering him to go easy on the outlaws he was forced to handle. Folks ought to always remember that when a man breaks the law, he's not entitled to a lot of pampering and petting, but that he forfeits his rights and considerations when he commits whatever crime it is that he's guilty of.

It hadn't been that way in Parsonville at the beginning, Royce recalled. When he took over from an elderly marshal who had permitted the hardcases to run wild, the town had welcomed his methods. There were no complaints as to his treatment of lawbreakers, and as a result of letting him do his job in his own way, Parsonville had quickly become a good, clean town.

But he guessed folks had forgotten all that, or maybe it was this thing they called progress. Dunn had told him one day that everything was changing—including the law—and matters pertaining to it, particularly enforcement, had to be looked at from a different angle.

Well, he'd thought at the time the mayor was telling him about it, that left him out in the cold. He knew only one thing—an outlaw was an outlaw and had to be treated as such. That was a fact as certain as white was different from black.

Raising an arm, Jake Royce brushed at the sweat on his forehead with the back of his hand. It was sweltering inside the office, and turning, he glanced at the lone window to be sure he had opened it. It was open, and sighing, he came back around to the desk.

He'd as well start clearing out his possessions, he decided. The result of the council meeting was a foregone conclusion, it seemed to him. Dunn had hinted broadly months ago that he'd best change his ways—or else. But Royce could think of no way he could do that and still get the job done the way he

21

figured he should, and so he had dismissed it from his mind.

The pile of dodgers was still before him, forgotten abruptly when Max Kastman's cry for help had reached him. Absently, he began to assemble and form them into a stack. He had been going through them, searching for the likeness of a man who had recently appeared in Parsonville and was staying at the hotel. Royce hadn't bothered to learn the stranger's name since outlaws, particularly the well-dressed, prosperous-looking ones such as the stranger, seldom if ever use the correct one.

Royce continued perusing the stack, found none of the pictures or descriptions matched the stranger. That, of course, was far from proof the man was no criminal since there were all too many on the loose that he did not have posters on.

He had to admit the stranger lacked the appearance of an outlaw, looked more to be a wealthy cattleman, or merchant. But appearances meant nothing any more; the day when all criminals were down-at-the-heel, dirty, unshaven tramps was past, if ever it really existed. Jake recalled that the worst killer he'd ever come up against had been a tall, handsome fellow who sported a silk hat, hard collar, and a cutaway coat.

Setting the stack of dodgers aside, Royce began to lay out the objects that were his—an old leather billfold; the star he'd worn down in south Texas before coming to Parsonville; letters from a friend back in Ohio—a woman whom he thought of now and then, occasionally with regret, but always with fondness; a half-full box of cartridges for the old Remington forty-four rifle that he still hung on to but never used any more.

Jake paused, stared at the snub-nosed shells, remembering how the weapon, wrestled from his grasp by a man spurred to desperation, was almost the source of his death. Stunned by a blow to the head, he had watched the rifle come up, saw the round, black hole of the muzzle center on his heart, and then heard the dry click as it misfired thanks to a faulty pin. He was able to get his pistol out in the next instant and bring the incident to an end.

Accumulating the items on the top of his desk, Royce started through the remaining drawers, claiming what was his and adding other articles to the pile. He had not decided as yet what he would do or where he would go when it was all over and done with; he simply had not gotten that far along with planning. Everything had come to a head so suddenly.

The lawman hesitated, glanced through the open doorway to the street, and listened idly to the sound of a passing carriage, its iron-tired wheels making a grating noise as they sliced through the sandy dust, while he gave the immediate future a bit of consideration. He'd hang around until morning, he reckoned, say so long to a few—a very few—people; and then load up his horse and ride out. He'd make up his mind then which direction he'd take.

Royce brought his attention back to his desk and the business of collecting his personal belongings, and then he looked again to the doorway as the thud of boot heels on the landing drew his notice. The entrance darkened, and the stranger he had thought might be an outlaw stepped inside.

'Marshal,' the man said in a level voice. 'I'm Riley McQueen. I'd like to talk to you.'

CHAPTER FOUR

Royce studied McQueen coldly. A man somewhere in his fifties, he had graying hair and mustache, dark, piercing eyes, and the expensive but serviceable clothing of a successful rancher.

'I'm not the marshal—leastwise I won't be after a bit,' Jake said 'If you've got some bellyaching to do, go talk to the mayor about it.'

McQueen shook his head. 'Know what happened down the street—and heard the talk. I reckon you're about to lose your star.'

'Seems—'

McQueen smiled. 'Guess it could be said that if it comes about, it'll maybe be all to the good far as I'm concerned.'

Jake Royce wiped at the sweat on his forehead, folded his arms across his chest, and considered McQueen narrowly.

'Mind laying that out? I don't savvy what you're getting at.'

'You will. I rode a far piece to talk to you, make you a proposition—but I expect I'd best tell you a little about myself first. Already spoke my name, Riley McQueen. Own a ranch over Texas way—the Q Bar. It's the biggest one in my part of the state.'

And likely the most prosperous, Royce

25

thought, looking more closely at McQueen as the man reached for one of the straight-back chairs ranged along the wall, drew it up near to the lawman's desk, and settled onto it. Looped across the front of the rancher's vest was a heavy link, gold watch chain from which was suspended a large diamond the value of which probably exceeded a lawman's salary for an entire year, perhaps more.

'So? What's that got to do with me?' Royce asked, a bit impatiently.

'Mostly to let you know that I'm able to do what I say I will—that I can hold up my end of any deal that I make with a man.'

Jake leaned back in his chair, puzzled. McQueen, beads of moisture standing out on his browned skin also, drew a white handkerchief from an inside pocket of his coat, mopped at his face and neck. Outside in the street the drumming of two riders loping by was a rhythmic beat in the stilled afternoon.

'Still ain't making no sense to me—'

McQueen hitched his chair a bit closer to Royce's desk. Loosening the buttons of his vest, and running a finger around the inside of his collar, he nodded.

'Just showing my openers, getting them out of the way. Can get down to business now.'

The lawman shrugged. His mood had not improved any in the last hour, and he'd as soon McQueen would take whatever business he had to hash over to Aaron Dunn, or someone else. Parsonville and its problems would soon be a part of his past and would be of no interest to him. Still, McQueen had said something about a proposition he wanted to make and—

'Like I said before, I came a long way to talk to you, Royce. Your reputation reaches out mighty far.'

Jake smiled bitterly. That reputation was costing him his job. 'Maybe, but the way I'm seeing it right now, it don't count for much.'

'Does with me—that's why I came looking for you. Had figured I might have some trouble hiring you away from your town marshal job, but you quitting maybe'll make it some easier.'

Royce shook his head 'Best you get it straight. I'm not quitting—I'm getting fired.'

'And that's on account of you using your gun, I take it.'

'Yep, that's it. The mayor, and I reckon most of the townfolks, figure I've been a mite too quick and handy with it.'

McQueen smiled. 'Hard to understand them. Where I come from a lawman killing off an outlaw is just fine with about everybody.'

'Was here—once,' Royce said, not in the mood to delve further into the matter with an explanation.

'And that's why they're wanting your badge?'

'That's why.'

'But it's not all just because of what happened out there a while ago—shooting those two outlaws that robbed the general store, I mean.'

'Only a part of it. Been coming on for some time. That shooting was like the last rock that broke the wagon down.'

'Understand one of them was a woman. You know that?'

'No, was no way to tell. She was dressed up like a man, and she come at me shooting . . . You mind getting to the point—why you rode all the way from Texas to talk to me?'

'Got a job for you—a sort of special one,' McQueen said, brushing at his mustache. 'I figure you're the only man that can handle it.'

A job. Royce mulled that about in his mind. A big, rich rancher coming a couple of hundred miles maybe, to hire him to do a job. That added up to only one thing: McQueen had somebody he wanted killed.

'You got any plans when you pull out of here?'

'Nope, haven't got around to making any yet. My belly's full of being a lawman—leastwise right now. Might just hang up my guns and go back home to Ohio.'

'You got family there?'

'Some, I think. It's mostly a woman I know. Or maybe I'll just ride for a spell, take a look at Arizona and California. I've never seen the ocean.'

'Takes a bit of money to go drifting around—'

'I've got a bit—not much, but I reckon there'll be enough.'

'A man never really has enough, the way I see it,' McQueen commented. 'Now, I don't know how well you're fixed or what you figure's enough, but the job I'm offering you will put you up in top shape for doing all you want for quite a time.

'And it's a job you can do easy. Saw you once, in Santa Fe. You'd gone there after some outlaw. He'd thrown in with a couple of friends, and they'd all holed up in a little 'dobe hut right off the plaza.'

Royce was digging into his memory, endeavoring to recall the incident. It was a vague shadow in the back of his mind, but as the rancher talked, it slowly came to him. It involved a killer, a cold-blooded murderer, in fact, who had knowingly shot down an unarmed man. He had been a deputy sheriff in a southern New Mexico settlement at the time and had trailed the man across the Territory, cornering him finally in the old capital city of Santa Fe.

'I recollect seeing you walk right up to the door of that shack, kick it in, and start shooting. Then when you figured you had your man, you started to go in after him; but a couple more of his pals showed up and decided to horn in. You'd already bolstered your gun and they had theirs out, but you drew and downed both of them. Was the fastest bit of gunplay I ever saw—and I never forgot it. Fact is, it's why I came looking for you.'

'For my gun, you best say,' Royce said dryly.

McQueen smiled. 'Yeh, I reckon you could say that—but it's because you're the best. There's plenty of gunnies I could hire—I've got one working for me right now—but I didn't give him a second thought. I don't figure he or any of the others are good enough to do the job I'm thinking about—'

'You've been a hell of a long time getting to the point, McQueen,' Jake cut in. 'I'll make it easy for you. Who do you want me to kill?'

CHAPTER FIVE

Riley McQueen laughed. 'Knew I was right, picking you.'

'Meaning you figured I was cold-blooded enough to do your killing for you—'

'Not exactly that,' the rancher said, sobering. 'What I meant was that it's a business—a profession with you, and there'd be no beating around the bush when it came down to who and why.'

'All depends,' Royce said, shaking his head. 'Haven't signed on with you yet.'

'The job'll pay you a thousand in gold when it's done. After that you can ride on— go back to Ohio or wherever it is that you've got a woman waiting, head on west for Arizona—or go to work for me as a troubleshooter. Pay for that's a hundred a month and keep.'

'What's a troubleshooter do?'

'Keeps my range clear of nesters and rustlers. Job'll fit right in with the kind of work you've been doing.'

Royce looked up. His cool, narrowed eyes met those of McQueen. 'Killing—that what you mean? Best I remind you that every man I've cut down was an outlaw, and I shot them only when I was forced to.'

'Well, the man I want you to take care of is just that—an outlaw . . . You want to go over to Brock's Saloon, and talk this over? It's mighty damned hot in here, and I'm dry as cotton. Could sure use a couple of drinks.'

Royce briefly considered the suggestion, shrugged, and drew himself upright. 'Suits me,' he said, and put on his hat.

The rancher, on his feet and moving toward the door, glanced back. 'You figure you're interested in the job?'

Jake hitched at the pistol on his hip and gave McQueen a humorless smile. 'Why not?' he replied, and followed the man out into the street.

Turning, they angled for the saloon, the best as well as the largest in the settlement. At once the lawman slowed, his glance going to and touching the dozen or so clusters of persons scattered along the way, some on the board sidewalks, others on the landings fronting business houses or in the yards of the few residences that were on the settlement's main street.

Farther on, at Aaron Dunn's feed store, Jake saw Tom Bell, Kastman, Doc Gossage, and a couple other men in a group facing the mayor. The council apparently was still in session, and Royce wondered if they were having trouble deciding his fate.

'Folks seem to be hashing things over pretty good,' McQueen said as they walked slowly through the driving sunlight toward Brock's. 'Could be you won't be out of a job.'

'You're wrong,' the lawman said dourly. 'If you was to listen to them I expect you'd find out they're figuring a way to ride me out of town on a rail. But they don't have any say-so on anything. It's that bunch down there in front of the feed store. They're the town council. It'll be them that settles it . . . One with the dude hat on's Dunn, the mayor.'

'No friend of yours, I take it—'

'Not any more,' Royce answered and paused.

They had reached the corner occupied by Charlie Brock's saloon, the sign across the front of which read, in somewhat faded letters: CHOICE OF LIQUOR, GAMBLING AND WOMEN. WELCOME ALL. Half a dozen men had gathered at the edge of the saloon's porch, and at the approach of Royce and the Texas rancher, conversation abruptly ceased.

Jake swept the silent party with a slow, contemptuous look. All had once been numbered among his friends, but now the aura of resentment toward him had spread like some virulent disease, infecting them all.

Folks can forget what a man does for them mighty soon, an old lawman laying aside his badge had once told him. *You're tall in the saddle with them when things are going to suit them, but do something that rubs them wrong and you'll find yourself about as popular as a polecat at a Sunday school picnic.*

He had laughed at the time, Jake recalled,

and told himself that he'd never let it happen to him. He'd do the kind of job people wanted and make them respect him for his honesty and ability.

He'd been young then, new at wearing a star, and all full of ambition and determination to be the best.

And, he reckoned, he had been—but what had it led to? His losing his star—and being offered the job to kill a man, thus becoming a hired gun. Royce turned his head, spat angrily into the loose dust.

'Can't say as I blame you for how you feel,' McQueen said. 'Man can bust a gut and risk his hide every hour of the day and night for damn little pay, and nobody ever really appreciates him doing it. I expect there's damn few around this town that you haven't done plenty for during the five years you've been the marshal.'

Royce frowned. 'How'd you know I've been here five years? Never mentioned it myself.'

The rancher smiled, looked off. 'Done some asking around—I'm careful that way. Always like to know what I'm doing and all about a man I aim to deal with. Keeps me from making mistakes.'

Jake made no comment but again let his gaze rake the men standing quietly on the walk waiting for him and the Texan to pass. McQueen was right; of the five there, three had called upon him, as marshal, for help. All had been exceedingly grateful and declared their eternal friendship. Now they were unwilling even to speak, were moved only to nod coolly.

'You're dead right,' he said, swinging his attention back to McQueen. 'Take this place—belongs to a man named Brock. When I pinned on my star, it was a hangout for cardsharps, grifters, whores, and two-bit outlaws on the dodge. They ran things pretty much to suit themselves, and Brock couldn't do anything about it.

'Asked me right off if I'd do what I could to clean out the place, get them off his back so's he could run his own saloon. It was like the hardcases owned it instead of him.'

'Can see you got the job done for him.'

'Yeh. Took some shooting, and a couple of the cardsharps ended up in the boneyard, but Charlie got his saloon back.'

'He one of them standing there on the walk?'

'No, he'll be one of them at the council meeting.'

'You figure he'll vote to turn you out?'

Royce pushed back his hat, swiped at the sweat above his brows with a wrist. 'He'll go with Dunn—and Dunn wants my badge.'

McQueen considered the meeting in front of the feed store thoughtfully. 'But what if the others don't side with Dunn? Could be they'll figure the town can't get along without you.'

'Not much chance of that. They all feel pretty much the same as the mayor—that it's come to the point where I'm keeping business away.'

'And that sure does hurt a counter-jumper!'

'Does, for a fact,' Royce agreed. 'But I reckon you can't blame them. When people don't come into town to buy, it's bad—and I suppose they figure they've got the right to get rid of the reason why.'

'That being you and your fast gun, in this case.'

'That's it. It's not something new that just popped up today. It's been sort of brewing for several months—ever since one of the big cattle outfits decided to bypass the town, buy their supplies and let their drovers do their hell-raising somewheres else. Parsonville—meaning me—was too tough on them, they claimed.'

They had reached the wide porch that extended across the front of the saloon, were climbing the steps that led up to it. A man sitting in a chair tipped back against the wall, rocked forward and got to his feet. He glanced at Royce, nodded slightly, and moving off the board flooring, entered the street where he joined the men at the corner.

'Ain't heard you say what you'll do if they don't take your star,' McQueen remarked.

'Not much chance of them not doing it,' Royce said, and then broke off abruptly, seeing

36

the councilmen, led by Aaron Dunn, coming toward them from the feed store. The meeting was over; the decision had been reached.

A hard smile pulled at the corners of Jake Royce's mouth as he turned completely around to face the approaching men. He waited until they had reached the center of the street and then, raising a hand, halted them.

'Can hold up right there,' he said. 'It's a hot day, and there ain't no use of you working up a sweat.'

'Marshal,' Dunn began, coming to a stop. 'The council's talked this matter over and we've decided—'

'No point in you wasting your breath either because I'm not interested. I've done some deciding myself. Best you get yourself another marshal, Mayor I've quit,' Jake Royce said, and unpinning his star, tossed it to the feed store man.

Wheeling, Jake nodded to McQueen. 'Let's get that drink and finish up our talking. I'm working for you now.'

CHAPTER SIX

A satisfied grin crossed McQueen's face. 'I'm sure glad to hear that, Marshal—or maybe I best start calling you Royce,' he said as they moved up to the doorway of the saloon and entered.

Back in the street a murmur of voices broke out. The men grouped at the corner were hurrying up to where Aaron Dunn and the other members of the council were standing, seemingly a bit confused at the sudden switch. Dunn, however, appeared relieved, as if he dreaded telling Jake Royce of the decision the council had come to and was thankful to be spared the necessity. The others, ill at ease, brushed aside the questions put to them, and as Royce and the Texas rancher disappeared into the saloon, they began to drift away.

'Who's this outlaw you're wanting me to cut down?' Jake asked, choosing one of the tables in the rear of the room and making his way toward it. Settling down onto one of its chairs, he beckoned impatiently to the bartender. His mood had changed little; there was still a bitterness in his tone, and his manner was abrupt and direct.

McQueen drew back the seat opposite him and sat down. Removing his hat, he again wiped at the sweat on his face and neck with the white handkerchief, tucked it into its pocket and, leaning forward, looked straight into Royce's half-closed eyes.

'Calls himself Monte Jackson,' he said. 'A real hardcase—tough and mean. He's mighty fast with a gun, so don't figure on it being a cinch.'

'Something I never do,' Royce said dryly. 'He wanted by the law for anything?'

'Expect so, but I don't know what.' McQueen leaned back as the bartender arrived with two glasses and a bottle, set them on the table, and turned away. 'Truth probably is that no lawman's got the guts to go after him if he is wanted. Just too risky.'

Jake filled the glasses, and without waiting for McQueen, tossed off his drink in a single gulp—noting the entrance of Charlie Brock into the saloon as he did.

'Works that way sometimes'

'But not for you, I reckon,' the rancher said. 'I doubt if you ever backed off bringing in a man no matter who he was.'

Royce let the compliment pass unnoticed. 'What's this Jackson done?'

'To me? Well, that's a personal matter I'd as soon not go into. Done plenty to others around my part of the country—the small ranchers and merchants and such.'

'Holdups, robberies—that what you're talking about?'

'And a couple of murders.'

39

Frowning, Royce gave that thought. Then, 'Seems to me the law would be doing something about that.'

'Jackson's smart enough to cover his tracks. I guess I could say that there's only a few of us knows what kind of a man he is.'

Royce shrugged, refilled his glass, paused to listen to the shrill laughter of a woman on the far side of the room.

'Looks to me like you could take care of him on your own,' he said, finally. 'Could make up a posse—'

McQueen's features darkened. 'We've got reasons why we can't do that—relatives looking for revenge, for one thing, and we don't want any of that,' he said, his voice impatient. 'Now, if you're going to be needing a reason for everything, maybe you better not take the job.'

'I set out to kill a man, I want to know why,' Jake replied coldly, and looked up as Brock halted beside the table.

The saloon owner, his manner apologetic, nodded to McQueen and then to Royce. 'Want you to know, Marshal, that I voted against turning you loose. So did a couple of the others—but it wasn't enough to override Aaron and the ones siding with him.'

'Obliged, Charlie,' Royce drawled. 'My friends all seemed to have died off plenty fast.'

Brock wagged his head. 'Usually the way it goes. You leaving town?'

40

'Tomorrow, probably.'

'Well, drop by before you go, and we'll have a couple of drinks for the road.'

Royce said, 'Sure,' and watched Brock retreat to the counter, step in behind it, and, acquiring an apron, take his place beside the bartender. The saloon was beginning to fill up, Royce saw, and realized the day was almost over and the night's business was beginning.

'You swallowing what he said?' McQueen wondered. 'About not voting against you, I mean.'

'Maybe. Makes no difference anyway. I'll be putting this town behind me.'

'That mean you're still aiming to take the job I've offered you?'

Jake drained the second shot glass of liquor, slowly poured another, his eyes on the amber colored liquid as it trickled from the thin neck of the bottle.

Accepting the rancher's offer put him squarely on a level with all other hired guns, he was realizing. Paid killers had always rated low on his scale of men, and the thought of becoming one of them was difficult to adjust to. All of his training as a lawman, all of the things that over the years had come to mean right in his mind, were contrary to what he was now agreeing to do, and something deep in his conscience was rebelling.

But the gun was his trade, his profession, he told himself. It was all he knew, and—since he had become proficient in its use—what was wrong with cashing in on that expertise?

He'd never killed a man who didn't have the same intention in mind toward him, so he was untroubled on that point; and, too, those who had gone down by his gun were outlaws and deserved a bullet. Logically, then, he should not hesitate to take on the chore Riley McQueen had offered him.

Monte Jackson was an outlaw, a killer, and a gunman of no mean ability. It was understandable that the rancher, who even now wasn't wearing a gun, and the others he spoke of, were reluctant to shoot it out with Jackson. A reputation such as the outlaw apparently had was intimidating to the average man, and hiring an outsider to rid themselves of his kind was fairly common practice.

Royce reckoned he was that outsider in this case. Riley McQueen, having seen him in action that time in Santa Fe, had remembered; and when the decision had been made by him and his friends to do something about Monte Jackson, he had ridden all the way from his Texas ranch to hire him.

But there was still that reluctance, that bad taste in Jake's mouth when he thought of becoming a hired gun. Still—what the hell? He was being paid to use his gun when he wore a star, wasn't he? As well be sheared for a sheep as a goat.

Royce started to speak, to assure the waiting

McQueen that he fully intended to take the job, and then he hesitated as three men, swaggering grandly from the effects of too much liquor, halted at the table. Jake knew them all well—cowhands from a ranch east of town who had been the source of much trouble until he had straightened them out.

'Sure going to be mighty nice, not having you around here, Royce,' one said. He was a squat, dark man with a heavy black beard and full mustache.

'Can't say as I'll be missing any of you either, Gabe,' Royce countered in a dry voice.

'There's a couple of little things I'd sure like to square up with you,' the taller of the three said. 'We're owing you, Marshal—and now that you ain't no marshal no more, I figure we ought to pay you off.'

'Goes for me, too,' the remaining man said thickly.

Royce smiled bleakly at McQueen. 'Some more of my friends,' he said, and rising suddenly, he seized the tall cowhand by the front of his shirt, swung him about, and sent him stumbling into his two friends.

'That what I think of your squaring-up idea, Pino,' he snapped. 'Now, you take Gabe and Kissler and get the hell out of my sight!'

Activity in the saloon had come to a quick halt as the unexpected explosion of violence and the attention of all present had shifted to Royce and the three men. As the cowhands staggered about, struggling to regain balance, Charlie Brock, a short club in his hand, and backed up by the bartender equipped with a bung starter, hurried up. Together they took charge of the belligerent cowhands and shepherded them none too gently to the door and out into the street.

Royce waited until Brock and the bartender had returned and then poured himself a drink. McQueen studied him briefly and then spoke.

'Reckon you know you're going to be running into jaspers with grudges pricking their hides—like them—pretty regular from now on. That star you wore made a lot of difference.'

'Wearing it also makes a man an easy target,' Jake said indifferently. 'Where'll I find this Monte Jackson?'

CHAPTER SEVEN

Relief filled Riley McQueen's small, dark eyes, and a half smile parted his lips. Sliding his empty glass toward the bottle of whiskey for a refill, he nodded.

'Glad to hear you ask—was beginning to have my doubts about you taking the job. Guess now we've got a deal.'

'I reckon we have,' Royce agreed. His tone and manner had not changed, continued in the same resigned, reluctant vein.

'He won't be hard to find,' McQueen said, retrieving his now full measure of liquor. Forearms resting on the table, he began to twirl the glass between the fingers of his right hand. 'Town's called Kiowa Springs. East of here and across the line, then south. It's about a three-day ride. Ever been there?'

Royce shook his head. Around them now the night in the saloon was well underway. A half-dozen men lounged at the bar, and most of the tables with their quartette of chairs were occupied. The clicking of cards, the smell of liquor, and a hazy film of smoke filled the warm air, mingling with the low, steady drone of voices.

'Don't recollect it.'

'Not much of a place,' the rancher continued, 'so you haven't missed anything. It's got a half-dozen saloons, four, maybe five, stores, a few cathouses—and not much else.'

'Lawman?'

'No, it ain't big enough for that. Now and then the county sheriff or one of his deputies rides by, sees if we've got any problems. Doubt if they'd do anything about it if we did.'

'They been told about Monte Jackson?'

Riley McQueen rubbed at his jaw, stared into his glass of whiskey. 'Yeh, expect they have. I'll have to admit I never did. Figured there wasn't no use, us being such a small bunch.'

'Up to a sheriff to do something about a problem like that—makes no difference how many people are being bothered by this Jackson. He live right there?'

'Close by. When you get to Kiowa Springs, go to Dundee's Saloon, and ask the bartender where you can find Jackson. He'll be able to tell you.'

'The bartender got a name or will he be the only one there?'

'Only one—but his name's Dave Ernshaw. You won't have no trouble finding him. When you figuring to head out?'

Royce shifted on his chair, reached for his empty glass and the bottle as if to serve himself another drink, but had second thoughts and pushed both away.

'In the morning. Got a few things to do.'

'Goodbyes to say, that it?'

'Not many of them,' Jake said flatly. 'It's that I've got a couple of bills to pay off. Won't take me long, so if you're thinking about us riding out together I—'

'Nothing I'd like better,' McQueen cut in, 'but fact is I've got some business to take care of down in El Paso, and it'll hold me up for a week or better. But I'll be back at the ranch by the time you've got the job done.'

'You want to meet me in Kiowa Springs and square up?'

'No, best you ride out to my place. It's about twenty miles or so from the town, east—but anybody can tell you how to get to the Q Bar. You just come by, tell me you've taken care of Monte Jackson, and I'll pay you off. You need any cash now? I'm willing to give you some in advance if you do—or if you're thinking I might welch on you.'

Royce shook his head. 'No need. I'll collect after I've done my job and earned'—he hesitated, grinned wryly—'earned my bounty money. And far as you welching on me—I doubt if it'd take much to find you.'

McQueen laughed. 'Not in Texas,' he said. 'Like to say so long, Royce, now that I've got this off my mind and we've made a deal. Neglected my business long enough,' he added, shoving back his chair, rising, and extending a hand. 'Be seeing you in a week or so.'

Jake took the rancher's hand into his own,

shook it solemnly. 'You pulling out tonight?' he asked, glancing to the open doorway. It was now full dark.

'Depends on how pert I'm feeling in a couple of hours, but chances are I'll wait till first light in the morning. Good luck.'

'The same,' Royce said, and releasing the Texan's hand watched him push his way through the crowd to the saloon's exit and disappear into the night.

Immediately Charlie Brock came out from behind the bar and across to the table. Royce glanced up as the saloonkeeper halted before him.

'You want something to eat, Jake?' he asked. 'Can have the cook rustle you up a bite.'

Royce said, 'No thanks, Charlie. Aim to do my eating later—right now this whiskey's doing me the most good.'

'The bottle's on the house,' Brock said, and then added: 'Want to say again that I was against letting you go. Far as I'm concerned, you're the best lawman this town ever had—or maybe will have.'

'Too good, it seems,' Royce murmured. 'I'm obliged to you for standing by me, anyway.'

'Was only right. You get yourself a good job with that rancher—whatever his name is?'

Jake Royce nodded, let it drop with that. Brock was curious, he could see, but somehow he couldn't bring himself around to telling the man, one he considered a fairly good friend,

48

that he had hired out as a gunslinger.

'When you leaving?' Brock asked after it became apparent he was getting no more information on the ex-lawman's future.

'Come morning,' Royce said, getting to his feet. 'Reckon I'd best be getting my gear together right now. See you later on.'

Brock stepped back, smiled. 'I'll be right here,' he said, and as Royce turned for the door, continued: 'Don't forget to drop by for that drink.'

Jake nodded, and coming to the doorway, stepped out onto the porch and halted. It was a fine, balmy evening after the driving heat of the day, and the moon, full breadth and shining like a great silver disc, was flooding the land with its mellow light, softening the harsh, cornered lines of Parsonville's structures and muting the ragged brush and rocks of the flats beyond—lending all a quality of mystery.

Ignoring the three men lounging against the front wall of the saloon, Royce crossed to the edge of the landing and descended the steps to the street. He was restless, unaccountably so, not sure in his mind what he wanted to do next—get to his quarters and finish collecting his belongings; drop by Minnie Griswold's house at the edge of town and say his farewells to her and her girls; or go over to the Home Cafe, tell Della Harper that he was leaving and enjoy, probably for the last time, one of her fine meals.

He decided on that, and doubling back, he started along the street for the restaurant, which stood some fifty yards or so on down the way. Likely Della would have locked up by that hour, but that posed no problem; he'd go to the rear of the place, knock in the special way that they had agreed upon, and be admitted.

'Marshal—'

At the quiet summons coming from the passageway lying between one of the lesser saloons and Tom Bell's Hardware Store, Royce stopped short.

'In the back. Tom wants to see you,' the speaker, hidden by the shadows, continued.

Wondering what it could be that the merchant had on his mind, Jake cut off the walk and started down the littered corridor for the cleared, alleylike area that ran behind the buildings standing on that side of the street. He supposed Bell wanted to inform him that he, too, had voted against taking his star and that he in no way felt the same as did Aaron Dunn.

Well, it no longer mattered, Royce thought, and Tom Bell needn't go to any trouble. Like as not this was the last time he'd ever see the hardware man or be in Parsonville, so there was nothing to be gained by a show of friendship and loyalty and—

Royce jerked to one side as a dark shape lunged at him from the blackness at the end of the building that housed the saloon. A curse ripped from his tight lips as a warning rocketed through him and he realized he had carelessly permitted himself to walk into some kind of a trap.

And then, as he sought to wheel, draw his gun, lights popped brilliantly before his eyes as someone struck him from behind with a club and sent him down to his knees.

CHAPTER EIGHT

Stunned, anger rushing through him in a giant wave, Royce lurched to his feet. The crouched shape of a man came at him from the side. Jake pivoted, swung a balled fist from the heels. The blow caught the man on the side of the head, dropped him flat on the sun-baked ground.

'Get him—dammit! Get him!'

The club came down again. Royce sensed rather than heard its swish. He threw up an arm, turned, took it on his shoulder. In that same instant he felt hands grip him as several men closed in upon him and began to wrestle him about as they sought to pin his arms to his sides. His head rocked as a fist connected solidly with his jaw, sending his senses reeling once more. All strength abruptly departed his muscles, and he went lax.

'We've got him!' he heard a voice declare exultantly, seemingly from a great distance.

'Take his gun,' another ordered. 'I'm aiming to settle this my way.'

Royce, struggling to clear his befogged mind, was conscious of his pistol being yanked from its holster, of hearing it strike the wall of the saloon as it was tossed aside. Then a hand pushed him roughly into the center of the alley where moonlight, escaping the oblong shadow of the buildings, formed a bright pool.

'All right, Gabe—he's all yours.'

Gabe . . . Jake had finally cleared his senses with a savage jerk, was now fully aware of the moment. He realized now what it was all about. The three cowhands who had come up to him while he was in Brock's—Gabe, Pino, and Kissler—were behind it. After collecting a few friends, they had laid a trap for him, and like a greenhorn, he had walked right into it.

'Better do some thinking about this,' he said in a low, hard voice from the center of the lighted area. Gabe and the others were little more than shadows in the darkness beyond its fringe. 'Could be biting off more'n you can chew.'

Pino, in his faintly accented voice, replied: 'I do not think so. You can no longer hide behind the star of a marshal—'

'Maybe so, but I'll warn you one more time, you best think this over.'

'You ain't nothing no more, Royce,' Kissler. stated flatly. 'You're just a ordinary jasper like the rest of us without that badge, and that leaves it open for us to bust you around like we want without getting throwed in—'

'Back off—all of you—' Royce said. 'Star or no star, I can handle the likes of you anytime it's needful.'

'The hell you can!' Gabe shouted and came charging out of the darkness.

Jake flung himself to one side, endeavored

53

to avoid a collision and at the same time deliver an effective blow to the cowhand's jaw as he lurched by. He failed on both counts. Gabe's long arms caught him about the middle, causing him to misjudge and carrying them both to the ground.

The shock of their solid contact with the hard earth broke Gabe's grip, and Royce, free, bounded to his feet. Anger was now a soaring flame within him, all of the pent-up frustration and rage that he'd bottled inside himself since his conversation with Aaron Dunn that afternoon now surging to the surface and making themselves known.

Sucking for wind, Royce spun and caught Gabe, still in the act of rising, full on the side of the head with a vicious left. Pain shot up his arm, and cursing, he jerked back. He disliked fighting with his fists for this one reason; it was too easy to break a finger or a wrist on a man's hard skull—and a crippled hand was something he could do without in his business.

Through the hanging dust he saw that Gabe was on his hands and knees, head hanging, mouth agape. Nursing his throbbing left hand with his right, and feeling no shred of compassion, he stepped forward, drove a booted foot into the cowhand's middle, and sent him sprawling. Immediately there followed the sounds of scuffling feet. Strong hands gripped Jake Royce and held him rigid.

'Come on, Gabe—we got him!'

Gabe, muttering curses, pulled himself to his feet. Staggering a bit, he knotted his fists and lunged at Royce. Jake tried to pull clear of the fingers locked to him, but there were too many. He gasped in pain and buckled forward as Gabe drove a blow into his belly. Royce groaned as another blow smashed into the side of his head.

Anger overriding the wave of giddiness the blow evoked, Royce flung his weight to the left, reversed, and rocked to the right. The hands clinging to him loosened, and a moment later he wrenched free. Yells went up as he rushed Gabe, met the man head-on. Then, standing almost toe to toe, they began to trade blows, both breathing hard, sweating heavily, and choking on the dust their booted feet had stirred into drifting clouds.

Abruptly Gabe went down. Royce wasn't aware of the blow he'd delivered that had caused it, so furious had been the exchange. It apparently had been one to the jaw that had caught the cowhand just right.

Again favoring his left hand, Jake took a step back, drawing deep to get wind in his lungs. He sagged to his knees as a club, or perhaps it was a gun butt—he never did know which thudded into the back of his skull and sent a wave of darkness through him.

He was barely conscious of falling, and it seemed only fleeting moments before the cloying darkness dissipated and he was again vaguely conscious. He realized he was lying flat on the ground, that several men were gathered around him. He started to rise, but a booted foot clamped down on his outflung arm while another man's boot pressed into the small of his back, pinning him firmly.

'He's come to,' a voice said. 'You sure you want to do this, Gabe?'

'You're damn right,' the squat cowhand answered. 'He done me plenty of misery—I'm paying him back.'

'But stomping a man's fingers! I don't think you ought to do that,' a strange voice commented doubtfully. 'Man's got to be able to make a living, and with his fingers all busted to hell, I—'

'I'll tell you one thing for certain,' still a different onlooker said, 'I ain't going to be around when he gets up—no, sir—not me!'

'Where's that rock?' It was Gabe, demanding, insistent, paying no attention to the doubtful members in the party.

Royce stirred again, tried to pull clear of the feet that were holding him down. He was fully conscious now and completely aware of what Gabe had in store for him.

'You do this and I'll kill you!' he said, spitting the dust from his mouth as he spoke.

'You ain't doing nothing,' the cowhand replied. 'And I'm fixing you good so's you can't never use that gun of yours again! Grab his hand, Kissler—hold it on that there rock.'

56

Struggling, Royce fought to keep his arm from being stretched full length, his fingers from being spread upon the slab of rock someone had provided; but prone, unable to move, he was powerless to do much. He felt his hand come in contact with the cool surface of the rock, his fingers spread across it.

Cursing, he tried again to break free. If Gabe succeeded in doing what he had in mind, it would be the end of his days as an expert with a pistol. He'd seen what a boot heel could do to a man's fingers when brought down upon them with savage force; it left them twisted and mutilated and usually totally useless. The dark shape of Gabe loomed over him.

Desperate, seizing one last hope, Jake resisted the natural impulse to jerk back his hand and threw all his strength into a forward thrust.

He felt pain sear up his arm, cursed wildly. A voice muttered, 'You done it—let's get the hell out of here,' and then there followed the quick thump of men hurrying off into the night.

CHAPTER NINE

Royce rolled to his back and sat up. The pain in his left hand was all but forgotten now that his right hand throbbed insistently. Hesitating briefly, now holding his right hand, Jake pulled himself to his feet. The sound of Gabe and his friends departing were no longer audible, and he turned about to face the moonlight where he could better see his injured hand.

It was numb and he was uncertain as to how badly crushed it might be. He moved his fingers, flinched at the pain, but he felt relief when he saw they were unharmed. That last, desperate move he had made—thrusting forward instead of pulling back—had saved them. Gabe's boot heel had come down on the back of his hand instead. But there could be severe damage to that area, too, he realized— and he also realized that he should lessen that possibility by getting immediate medical treatment.

Moving toward the saloon, he searched about until he found his pistol and, sliding it into the holster, headed back up the passageway for the street. He'd first pay a visit to Doc Gossage and get his hands taken care of, then he'd hunt down Gabe and carry out the threat he'd made. It was a cold, rational decision; he had warned the cowhand of the consequences of his act, and he fully intended to make good his promise.

The office of the physician, a small cottage facing the street, was dark. Gossage was out, either on a call to a patient—which could be a person anywhere within a ten-mile radius of the settlement—or he had gone home.

Making the ride to the doctor's residence was impractical, as he lived at the edge of what was known as Vicker's Lake, a small body of water along which the better families had built homes so that they might be well away from town. It would be a long ride to the lake, and he'd have no assurance that Gossage would be there when he arrived.

Frowning, clutching his throbbing right hand with the left, which now merely ached, Royce glanced along the street. It was all but deserted, with most of the business houses, excepting the saloons, completely dark. A group of men were standing in front of Brock's, and a solitary rider on a tired horse came in from the north road and pulled up to the hitch rack fronting the saloon. Royce let his gaze drift on, come to a halt on the Home Cafe. Moonlight lay against its small, white-curtained window, starkly pointing it up.

Della Harper! Why hadn't he thought of her? She was just about as good as a doctor in most instances, having patched him up several times before when Gossage wasn't available or he figured his injuries weren't serious enough to call in the physician.

Wheeling, Royce cut back through the passageway to the area behind the buildings and crossed to the rear of the restaurant. He could see light rimming the sides of the shade, pulled down to block the window; he knew the woman would be there. Halting at the door, he rapped gently with his left hand—twice and then once.

There was the sound of a chair scraping against the floor, the chink of metal as a key was turned in a lock. The door swung inward and Della Harper, her figure silhouetted by the lamplight filling the room, stood before him.

'Jake! I was wondering if—' she began and broke off abruptly when she got a closer look at him—dusty, face smeared with blood, one hand cradling the other. 'Come in—come in!' she finished hurriedly, and stepped back to admit him.

Royce entered the room, sat down at the table where he had enjoyed coffee and pie and many meals, along with much pleasant conversation, with the woman. Although he was always conscious of her femininity, there was nothing stronger than a friendship—born of a man's need for woman and a woman's need for man—between them.

'How bad hurt are you?' Della asked, crossing to the small stove she used for cooking on the days when she did not open the restaurant.

'Reckon I've seen better days,' he replied, exhibiting his battered hands.

Her lips tightened, and then lifting one of the stove's lids, she dropped wood into the firebox, sprinkled in a bit of coal oil to hasten ignition, struck a match, and touched off the flames. As they leaped to life, she set a kettle of water over the opening, first taking a moment to wet a wash cloth. Then she pivoted toward Royce. Wiping the blood and dust from his face, she knelt before him and examined both injured hands.

'Fingers on this one's swelled a bit, but I don't think there's anything serious,' she said of one, and then fell to inspecting the other. Her brow drew into a frown. 'This one's been mashed! How did you—'

'Gabe Custer—him and a few of his sidekicks, ganged up to even the score for times past,' Royce explained. 'Not wearing a star makes a mighty big difference.'

'I heard about what the council did to you, Jake. I'm sorry.'

He shrugged, watched her rise and cross the room to a dome-lid trunk. Opening it, she took out a strip of white cotton cloth and began to rip it into strips.

Tall, slender, wearing a high-necked dress that came completely down to her ankles, Della looked more to be a nurse than the proprietor of a restaurant, he thought. Her hair was a soft brown, which matched her eyes; and while her features were small and regular, she did not possess beauty.

The kettle lid had begun to clatter as the steam rising from the now boiling water pressed against it. At once Della took up a small wash pan, filled it from the kettle, and placed it on the table before Royce.

'Let it cool a bit, then I want you to put both hands in it,' she directed. Then she left the room, returning shortly with a bottle of blue liquid.

Pouring a quantity into the container, she delayed for a minute or two, and then nodded. 'Try it, see if you can stand it. The hotter the better.'

Royce lifted his hands, allowed them to sink into the pan. The water was almost too hot, but he was mindful of her advice, and jaw clamped tight but cursing silently, he endured the near scalding.

'You're lucky your fingers, didn't get broken,' Della said, moving to the cabinet near the stove and obtaining cups and saucers.

'Had sense enough to look out for them,' Jake said. Beads of sweat were standing out on his forehead and he was grimacing with pain. 'Moved my hand just in time.'

Della, setting a pot of coffee over the fire to warm, considered him frowningly. 'How—how did they manage—'

'I let myself get suckered into a trap,' Royce

said in disgust before she could complete her question. 'Was in the alley behind Bell's Hardware. Was told Tom wanted to see me. Went there and they jumped me. Gabe and me went at it for a couple of minutes, then a couple of them held me down while he stomped me with his heel.'

Della shuddered, shook her head as if finding it difficult to believe men could do such a thing. Filling the two cups with the now ready coffee, she returned to the table, placed them on its oilcloth-covered surface, and sat down.

'Your hands feeling better?' she asked, taking him by the wrists and lifting them from the pan. The flesh of each had turned a bright red from the heat, but there was only a little swelling in both.

'Both pretty good,' he said. 'Sure have quit hurting like they were. I'm obliged to you, Della.'

She smiled, took up her coffee, sipped at it. Then, 'What will you do now that you're not the marshal here any longer?'

'Got myself a job working for a rancher over in Texas,' he answered, but went no further—unwilling, as he had been with Charlie Brock, to go into detail.

'I see.' Della's voice was low, quiet, and a sort of remoteness had come over her. 'When will you leave?'

Royce had lowered his hands into the

solution again, was flexing his fingers, testing their response. 'Tomorrow, I reckon, after I've—'

Somewhere along the street a gunshot flatted hollowly. Instantly Royce reacted and started to rise. And then with a wry smile at the woman, settled back. Such was no longer any affair of his.

'I reckon it's a habit,' he said.

Della shook her head, ignored his comment. 'After you've—what? You didn't finish.'

'After I've taken care of Gabe. Told him flat out I'd kill him if he stomped my hand. He went ahead anyway. I ain't figuring to let him get by with it.'

Della was staring at him. 'You—you're really going to kill him?'

Royce nodded, removed his left hand from the pan of water, and taking up his cup of coffee, raised it to his lips. 'I warned him. He didn't listen.'

'But to go out and kill him, Jake! You make it sound so offhand, so unimportant—'

Frowning, Royce drained the cup and set it back on the table. He was somewhat surprised by the woman's question and, after considering it briefly, shook his head.

'Reckon I never thought about it in that way. Was always just part of my job.'

'A part of it, maybe, when there was no other way out—but to just say you're going out and kill a man, why, that's murder!'

64

Royce withdrew his other hand from the pan of water, and pushed back from the table. 'You're starting to sound like Aaron Dunn and some of them others,' he said stiffly. 'I didn't make the rules—I just try to go by them best I know how . . . Obliged to you for fixing up my hands.'

'Don't you dare move I'm not finished doctoring you yet!' Della snapped. 'And maybe Aaron's right. Have you thought of that?'

'No. And since I'm through with him and this town, I don't aim to.' Jake paused, looked closely at the woman. 'You figure he's right?'

Della's shoulders stirred. 'I don't hold with killing—I'll tell you that much. But I do know that it's unavoidable at times, that a lawman like yourself doesn't always have any other chance except using his pistol.'

'That's the way it's been,' Royce said, settling back. 'Anytime I had to cut a man down was because he was trying to kill me first. Goes for the Yarbro girl and her husband. They both came shooting. I'm sorry about her, about both of them, but I wasn't about to stand there and get the hell shot out of me.'

'I understand that—and I think most people around here do. It's only that there's been so many times when you didn't have a choice—'

Royce swore deeply in disgust, again started to rise. Della laid a restraining hand on his wrists, smiled. 'I'm sorry, Jake. I'll say no more about it . . . Have you had your supper yet?'

65

Royce hesitated a moment and then grinned. 'I reckon I am a mite hungry. Just never got around to eating.'

'Then just set back and keep your hands soaking in that solution while I fix you something. There's some good stew that only needs heating up, and I made fresh light bread today along with berry pie.'

'Sure sounds good,' Royce said. 'Then I best be about my business.'

Della had risen, was now at the stove making preparations for a meal to set before him. 'Meaning Gabe Custer?'

An expression of annoyance pulled at the flat planes of Jake Royce's face. 'What I mean.'

'Well,' Della said, placing her hands on her hips and wheeling to face him, 'I'd better tell you this: you saved your fingers from being crushed, but your hand will be stiff and sore for several days. I'd not plan on making much use of it—like shooting a pistol. I doubt you'll be able to hold one tight for a while.'

Royce swore again in a low voice, stared at the floor unseeingly. 'Guess that settles that,' he muttered. 'I'll just have to look Gabe up later—maybe make a special trip back to take care of him. How long you figure it'll take for my hand to get back in shape?'

'Three or four days, at least, before the soreness is gone. I'm no doctor, but that's my guess.'

Jake's thoughts had shifted to Riley

McQueen and the job the rancher was paying him to do. By being careful and exercising his fingers, he reckoned his hand would be in shape again by the time he reached Kiowa Springs. And that was of utmost importance; he couldn't go up against a gunman such as Monte Jackson was said to be with a crippled hand.

'Best thing you can do, Jake Royce, is eat your supper and stay right here for the night where I can keep an eye on you,' Della said, sternly. 'We can keep soaking your hands, help them both along as much as possible before you ride out in the morning.'

Royce grinned. Della wasn't fooling him. What she had in mind was keeping him away from Gabe Custer—which he guessed wasn't such a bad idea considering the condition he was in.

'Suits me fine,' he said, and settled back in his chair once more.

CHAPTER TEN

Royce left Della Harper's place early that next morning. His left hand was back to normal, thanks to the treatment it had received, but while the soreness was all but gone from the right hand, the fingers were stiff; and when he closed them, as he would in holding a pistol, there was considerable pain.

In the matter of Gabe Custer, he had accepted by then, grudgingly, the conclusion he'd come to that previous evening; he'd return later and settle with him. Getting to Kiowa Springs and taking care of Monte Jackson as he'd promised was the important thing now. He'd told McQueen that he'd leave that morning, and it was a three-day ride, more or less. The rancher was expecting to be there within that time span.

Moving along the shadowy alleyway with a saffron sunrise flaring the east, Royce hurried to his quarters at the jail. Entering, he went immediately to work, thrusting the sack of lunch Della had prepared for him, along with a few pieces of extra clothing that he felt were serviceable, into one of his saddlebags.

Going then to the office area of the building, he collected the items that were of interest and necessary to him—extra cartridges, his spare pistol, a few letters and such—and dumped them into the other leather pouch. Hanging the bags over a shoulder, he took his rifle from its place in the wall rack, gathered up his slicker, and carried all to the small stable behind the jail where he kept his horse.

Saddling the white-stockinged black gelding, Jake slid the rifle into the boot, hung the saddlebags in their place, and then, as he started to tie down the slicker behind the cantle, remembered he would have need of a blanket. Returning to his quarters, he jerked the woolen cover off his bunk, retraced his steps to the stable, and wrapping the blanket inside the slicker, secured the cylinder into its place on the hull.

The sun was just breaking the horizon when he led the black out into the small corral that fronted the stable; but Parsonville was now awake and coming alive. Smoke was twisting upward from many chimneys as housewives prepared the morning meal for their families. Somewhere a cow lowed impatiently, and crows, streaming raggedly by overhead on their way to the fields east of town from the groves of trees in the west, were filling the warm, soft air with their raucous complaining.

Royce stood for a long minute in deep thought, his lean shape rigid in the rising light, hat tipped forward on his head, one hand grasping the black's reins, the other hanging idly at his side.

It was early, but there were a couple of persons he should see before leaving. One was Minnie Griswold, always a friend and a good listener when he had a troublesome problem plaguing his mind or a need to relax. The other was old Henry Tinnin who ran the livery stable. He owed Henry a few dollars for the care he'd given the black—and a man should pay his bills before he rides out even if he does plan to return, for there is always the possibility that he might encounter circumstances that will prevent him from coming back.

Turning to the gelding, and favoring the injured hand wrapped in a white strip of bandage, which Della had soaked in a solution that she said would heal the tenderness, Jake swung up onto the saddle. Settling himself, he started to wheel, but jerked the black to a halt.

Down the alley behind the buildings, four men had emerged from one of the small, less popular saloons. It was Gabe Custer, his two friends Kissler and Pino, and a man Jake did not recognize. They stood there in a tight group, laughing and talking about something—possibly the encounter with him, Royce thought grimly.

Anger stirred through him. They were plenty bold and brave, believing they had put him—now an ordinary citizen without the authority of his star—out of the way. As far as Gabe and the others knew, his fingers had

70

been crushed to pulp and his days of wielding a pistol with expertise were over.

Gabe thought as much! Royce smiled crookedly. Gabe Custer would find out different—maybe not right then, but a day not too far in the future would come. It could be a little more than a week, perhaps two—but the time would sure as hell come when Gabe would realize not only that he'd made a mistake, but that he was going to pay with his life for it.

It would be murder, Della Harper had insisted. He would no longer have the protection of his star if he used his gun—which led him to believe that Della, while unaware of it perhaps, was following the same line of thought that Aaron Dunn and a few others subscribed to. It was as if she were saying that his badge of authority did give him the right to kill, and now that he no longer possessed that authority, his shooting it out with another man—and surviving—would be murder. He wondered how she would feel about his hiring out to kill Monte Jackson.

He didn't need the power of a lawman's star to shelter his gunplay—if ever he did. He simply used his weapon as a tool of his profession, just as a carpenter used a hammer; only he was up against deadly opponents seeking to kill him, and his tool had to be more decisive.

It would feel good to settle with Gabe right

then and there—but it would be dangerous to draw and hold a pistol, and he was not the kind of man to pot-shoot another with a rifle. He'd wait until they could face each other on equal footing; and during that time maybe Gabe, thinking about the promise that had been made, would start to worry about it a little and sweat a whole lot, wondering when and where he'd unexpectedly be confronted.

Shrugging, and throwing a final glance at the men still conversing behind the saloon, Royce cut the black about, rode alongside the building that contained marshal's office, jail, and living quarters, and reached the street. Crossing over, he continued on to the livery stable.

Henry Tinnin was not yet there, the hostler informed him, and likely would not put in an appearance for another hour. Jake handed the overalled man the money he owed to the stableman, left the message that he would be gone for a spell but would return, and rode on.

Coming to the end of the street, Royce veered to his right and followed the dusty, weed-overgrown path to Minnie Griswold's house, a two-story, shutter-windowed structure set upon a slight hill.

Circling around to the rear, which was customary procedure for the regular patrons, Jake drew up at the hitch rack, dismounted, and ground-reining the black, climbed the steps to the back door landing. Entering, and familiar with the place, he walked the length of the hallway to the parlor.

A scantily clad girl, stretched out on a pillowed sofa, rose to greet him. 'Morning, Marshal,' she said.

He nodded. 'Morning, Trixie. I'm looking for Minnie.'

The girl smiled, pointed to the upper floor. 'She's entertaining a gentleman caller, Marshal.'

Royce shrugged. He was too early for everyone, it seemed. 'Trixie, I want you to give her a message for me. Tell her I've gone out of town for a spell but that I'll be back.'

'Sure, Marshal,' the girl said, and settled back on the sofa.

'And I'm not the marshal anymore. There'll be a new one, likely in a day or two.'

'Yeh, I know. Was you killing that poor girl and her man that got you kicked out.'

Anger and impatience stirred through Jake. He brushed it off. What the hell was the use? He'd always wear that brand, he supposed, where the people of Parsonville were concerned.

'Just don't forget to tell Minnie what I said,' he cautioned sternly, and pivoting, returned to his horse.

Mounting, Royce doubled back through the clumps of rabbitbush and globular snakeweed, and reaching the road that led south out of town, he swung onto it. Eyes straight ahead, he continued until he reached a slight rise and halted there. Twisting about, he had a last look at Parsonville.

It had been a good town for him despite the opposition he had encountered in the past year or so, and he'd been proud to wear the star of its marshal. True, he'd made but few friends, chief among them Della Harper; the saloon owner, Charlie Brock; and Minnie Griswold. But Jake was not a friend-making man, and he had no regrets. By the very nature of his calling, he was a loner.

Settling back in the saddle, Royce raked the gelding with his spurs and moved on, eyes now following the road as it unfolded ahead of him like a gray-brown ribbon, rising and falling over the low hills and winding in and out of the scattered stands of stunted trees.

He rode slowly, easily. There was no need to hurry as he had gotten off at the time planned, and pushing the black hard would be to no good purpose. It was said to be about a three-day ride to Kiowa Springs, and there was no point in trying to make it in less. Besides the—

Royce drew up short, almost bringing the gelding to his back legs. Three riders with pistols drawn and leveled had appeared abruptly from behind a clump of cedars. They closed in quickly, one meeting him face on, the two others circling around to get behind.

'Set quiet, Marshal—and raise your hands.'

Royce complied slowly. Eyes narrowed, he studied the man doing the talking. There was something familiar about him: lean, dark, a hard line for a mouth, and small, mean eyes. A Yarbro, he thought—one of the sons. He vaguely recalled seeing him in town a year, maybe two years ago.

'We're the Yarbros,' the rider said as if to confirm Royce's thoughts. 'Was heading into town after you. Bumping into you here saves us the trouble.'

CHAPTER ELEVEN

Royce stiffened as a warning rushed through him, filling him with a sharp wariness. Here was trouble: three brothers seeking vengeance for the death of their sister—and he with a crippled hand. But he showed no signs of apprehension.

'So,' he said quietly, 'you're the Yarbros. What the hell's that to me?'

'Plenty. Was you that killed my—our—sister, Nellie. Shot her down like a dog. You claiming you didn't?'

'No,' Royce replied evenly. 'Was me. She robbed a store, beat up the old man who owned it—then tried to shoot it out with me.'

'She wouldn't've done all that,' Yarbro stated flatly. 'Was that no-account man of hers, but not her.'

'She was in on it, was handling a gun same as him . . . Which one of the boys are you?'

Yarbo gave that thought, shook his head 'Can't see as it counts for nothing where you're headed, but I'm Dallas. That there's my brother Will,' he added, jerking a thumb at a dark, heavyset man, 'and the kid there, he's Saul . . . Get his gun and belt—that rifle, too, Will, and let's get cracking. Ma's waiting for us to bring—'

'No,' Royce cut in coldly, 'I'm not going

76

anywhere with you. Can say I'm right sorry about your sister, but she had no business throwing in with an outlaw.'

'Now, you're coming with us all right!' the youngest Yarbro, wiry, also dark, and with a sullen cast to his features, declared angrily. 'Could be we'll have to drag you at the end of a rope, but you're coming.'

'He's right,' Dallas said, 'so there ain't no sense in you putting up a fuss. Was a friend told us all about the killings, so we got you dead to rights. He said the town took your job away from you on account of it. That for true?'

Jake nodded, let his aching arms lower a trifle to ease the strain on them and lessen the throbbing in his injured hand.

Dallas Yarbro's mouth tightened and his shoe-button eyes glittered. 'I reckon that proves you hadn't ought've done it that you ain't nothing but a gun crazy killer, like folks say.'

Royce, remaining icily calm, said, 'Not it at all. That was only part of the reason. Trouble between me and the mayor's been building for a long time. Anyway, I've told you just how it was—that your sister and her husband were trying to kill me. Was nothing I could do but shoot back. Besides, it was my job.'

Dallas glanced at his brothers, spat. 'From what we been told, you figure it's your job to shoot down anybody that don't hop when you holler frog—'

'That's a damned lie!' Royce broke in, anger finally surfacing. 'Any time I used my gun it was because I had to . . . Now, get the hell out of my way! I've got a job over in Texas waiting for me, and it's a long ride.'

'You ain't goin' nowheres, mister, 'cepting with us,' Dallas said coldly, motioning at his brothers. 'You collecting his shooting gear—or ain't you?'

Jake, arms still raised under the threat of the elder Yarbro's pistol, heard the quick thud of hoofs as Will and Saul moved in beside him. One jerked the rifle from its boot while the other, Will, unbuckled the gun belt and swung it clear of his waist. Almost at the identical moment, Royce felt a rope drop about his shoulders. He reacted instantly. Rocking to one side, he threw himself off the saddle.

He struck the ground solidly, pivoted, caught Will Yarbro by the arm and pulled him off his saddle. They went down together, locked in each other's arms, both struggling to break free and deliver a telling blow. Jake, favoring his bandaged hand and heaving for wind, managed to get a knee up, drive it into Yarbro's belly. Will gasped in pain, loosened his grip. Immediately Jake lunged upright and, forgetting his injured hand, drove a hard blow to the man's jaw.

An involuntary yell of pain exploded from his lips as he recoiled. He fell back a step or two, blinded by dust and wracked with a thousand burning needles stabbing at his hand. Will Yarbro loomed suddenly before him, charging straight on.

'Saul! Get down there and help your brother!'

Royce barely heard Dallas Yarbro's shouted command as he pulled to one side to avoid the onrushing Will. He was only partly successful. The squat brother, arms flung wide, caught him with groping fingers as he lunged by. Jake, now fully mindful of his throbbing hand, was yanked half around, went off balance and down to his knees. In the next fragment of time, a blow to the back of his head sent his senses reeling. Saul had entered the fight, he realized numbly.

'Get him up! Get him on his feet!' Royce heard Will Yarbro's voice as if from a great distance. 'I owe that sonofabitch—and I aim to pay off!'

Senses still drifting, Jake felt himself being dragged to his feet. Hands locked to his arms, pinned them behind his back. Blinded by dust and sweat, he shook his head, endeavoring not only to clear it; but to see. His glazed eyes saw Will, lips pulled back over broad teeth in a mirthless grin, draw back his knotted fist. He was vaguely aware of the blow coming, sank to his knees as it caught him on the jaw and shattered his consciousness once more.

'Let him be,' Dallas ordered as Saul started to drag Royce upright again. 'He's had

79

enough. Besides, he best be alive when Ma sees him.'

Jake, senses again hovering listlessly about him and strength gone, allowed himself to go limp when Saul released his grip, and he sprawled full length onto the ground.

'Get that rope back on him,' Dallas directed. 'And you best tie his hands. I don't want no more trouble out of him.'

Royce was yanked to a sitting position. One of the Yarbros—he was too dazed to note which—pulled his arms together in front of him and bound his wrists, using a strip of rawhide. Again the rope, shaken off during the scuffle, was dropped about him; but this time the loop was quickly drawn tight.

'Get him on his horse—'

Both Will and the younger Saul, one supporting him at each side, hauled him to his feet and, propelling him to where the black stood, boosted him onto the saddle.

'Ain't sure he's going to stay there,' Saul said, jamming Royce's booted feet into the stirrups. 'He's kind of knocked out.'

'Up to him,' Dallas replied indifferently. 'He falls off, he'll have to walk or get drug all the way to the ranch.'

'Me and Will can sort of ride alongside, prop him up—'

Dallas hawked, spat into the brush. 'Nope, he figures himself to be a real tough bastard. Let him take care of hisself. Anyhow, I got something else for Will to do.'

The squat Yarbro, preparing to swing up onto the saddle, paused, glared at his older brother. 'You sure'n hell've took it on yourself to be high and mighty,' he observed, sourly. 'You're giving orders like some section boss. Ma give you the right?'

'Me being the oldest gives me the right,' Dallas replied coolly. 'But it don't make a damn to me. I can send Saul—or go myself.'

Will completed his mounting and settled himself in the saddle. 'Go where?'

'To Parsonville. Got to get Nellie. She'll be at the undertaker's.'

'It going to cost anything?'

'I don't know—but don't pay him nothing. Tell him we never told him to get her. Can say we take care of our own without nobody outside the family sticking their nose into it. He gives you any back talk, just you tell him I'll ride in and straighten it out.'

'How'll I get her back to the ranch? Don't seem right hanging her crossways on my saddle.'

'Borrow a wagon from the livery stable. I expect them folks in town are feeling real ashamed over what happened to Nellie, and they'll want to be nice to us and help all they can.'

Will nodded, started to pull away, halted. 'What about Luke? You want me to bring him back, too?'

81

'Hell no—let the town bury him!' Dallas said, motioning at Saul to take the reins of Jake Royce's horse and pull out. 'You go toting him back to the ranch and Ma'll feed him to the hogs . . . Don't take no more time'n you have to, now.'

'A mile's a mile,' Will grumbled, moving off. 'I'll do the best I can, but there ain't no way a man can make one shorter.'

CHAPTER TWELVE

Despite the grogginess, Jake Royce heard and understood all that passed between the Yarbro brothers as he was being trussed up and loaded onto his horse. And then as they moved off, the black being led by Saul with Dallas at his side, his mind gradually cleared completely and began to function as it should.

One fact was dead certain—he was in a hell of a tight. The Yarbros meant to exact vengeance upon him for the killing of Nellie, and tied up as he was, there wasn't a damn thing he could do about it . . . At least for the time being, he consoled himself. A man was alive until he was dead—and the Yarbro clan were going to find out that he was a hard one to kill.

His hand was throbbing continuously, had been since he'd thoughtlessly driven it into Will Yarbro's jaw, and with one hand bound tight to the other as it was now, the pain had doubled. But Royce said nothing, knowing he would receive no sympathy, and simply maintained a deep silence as they rode steadily toward a line of brown hills well to the southwest.

The Yarbros, too, were quiet, only a few words passing between them from the time they departed the point where he had encountered them to when they rode into the littered yard of the ranch.

Ranch . . . it was more a sharecropper's ramshackle farm than a ranch, Royce thought as they pulled to a halt at the sagging crossbar of a hitch rack near a corral. The house, he noted, was small, square, made entirely of wood, and had a sharply slanted roof.

The door—the one visible in the front wall—was of warped planks; it hung from leather hinges and opened out rather than in, which led Jake to believe the structure had been a shed prior to being elevated to the status of a residence. The single window nearby contained but half a glass pane, the lower part being covered with an animal skin of some kind that had been scraped thin to admit light.

Chickens and hogs roamed the premises at will, and in the entrance of a makeshift leanto shed at the rear of the yard could be seen a solitary cow, her head low as she methodically chewed her cud while considering their arrival

'Climb down,' Dallas directed, dismounting and stepping up beside Royce.

Jake threw a leg over the black's neck, took a moment to balance himself, and then kicking his other foot free to the stirrup, slid to the ground.

'Here comes Ma,' Saul announced from nearby.

Royce turned, put his attention on the

slatternly woman approaching from the house. Dressed in a soiled black skirt, faded shirt, gray hair hanging raggedly about her head in wayward wisps, she had a set, narrow face and the same small, cruel eyes of her son Dallas.

'You got him, eh?' she said, wiping her hands on the slack of her skirt.

'Yeh, Ma, we got him,' Dallas replied.

'Didn't take you long,' the woman said, folding her bony arms and fixing Royce with a cold stare.

'He was pulling out—headed for Texas. We jumped him on the road a ways from town. Like that drummer said, they took his job away from him.'

Ma Yarbro nodded slowly, her hard, hate-filled eyes never straying from Jake Royce. Abruptly she drew back her head, spat into his face. Anger flamed through Royce. He lunged forward, linked fists upraised to club the old harridan. Dallas, holding the rope that encircled Jake's shoulders, jerked it taut, checking the onetime lawman's impulsive motion.

'That done me a powerful lot of good,' the woman said.

Royce, a contemptuous smile on his lips, shrugged, wiped his face with a sleeved forearm.

'You're a murdering bastard—killed my Nellie.'

'I shot her, if that's what you mean,' Jake

85

replied calmly. 'Had to, or get myself killed.'

'Claims her and Luke was shooting at him,' Dallas volunteered.

The old woman spat again, this time to the ground. 'I reckon that's a lie. Nellie'd a hit you had she been shooting at you.'

'One thing's sure,' Saul pointed out, 'him getting fired on account of what he done proves he didn't have no call shooting them.'

Ma Yarbro sniffed, placed her hands, worn and knotted, on her hips. 'That Luke had it coming. Never was worth nothing, so it don't matter hog leavings about him. I should've blowed him to hell the day he come here sparking Nellie. Knew then he'd get her into trouble—and that's just what he went and done.'

'Nellie made up her own mind, Ma,' Dallas said, shrugging. 'Ain't no call for you to go blaming yourself. If you'd a'set down on her like as not she'd've just up and run off with him.'

'And maybe if she had, I'd sent you boys after them and drug them back! But I ain't one to bawl once the stew's been ruined. What's done's done . . . You send Willie to fetch her back?'

'Sure did, Ma,' Dallas said. 'Told him not to pay them counter-jumpers nothing, just borrow a wagon and load her up and head back. He ain't bringing Luke. I figured you wouldn't want—'

86

'I don't want him—dead or alive—within a hundred miles of my place!'

'That's just what we figured,' Dallas said, and nodded at Royce. 'What do you want me to do with him?'

'What you'd best do,' Jake said before the woman could answer, 'is turn me loose. I was only doing my job, and you getting back at me for that'll only lead to big trouble for you—from a U.S. marshal.'

'Is that so?' Ma Yarbro said scornfully. 'Ain't nobody knows you're here—and I don't reckon there's anybody that'd care from what we was told last night by that peddler who dropped in. And you ain't a lawman no more, so no U.S. marshal's going to give a hoot about you.'

'You're wrong there,' Royce said. 'When I don't show up in Texas when I'm expected, they'll figure something's wrong and start looking for me.'

'Well, they won't find you,' the old woman drawled, winking broadly at Dallas and Saul 'Leastwise not unless they got some prairie dog friends that'll do a powerful lot of digging for them.'

Saul pushed his hat to the back of his head and rubbed at his sweaty jaw. 'I ain't so sure that he ain't right, Ma. He's known pretty good around here, and somebody could come hunting him. Maybe we best—'

'We're doing just what we talked about last

night,' the woman broke in stubbornly. 'He murdered Nellie, and that gives us the right to hang him, just like the law'd do to one of you boys was you to shoot down some poor girl . . . Now, stash him in the shed—fix that door good! We'll take care of him after we've had services over Nellie and got her buried. Be more fitting then.'

Ma Yarbro wheeled, her sudden movement catching several hens unaware and sending them fluttering wildly off to one side. Dallas grasped Royce by the shoulder, spun him about, and shoved him roughly toward a small shed standing nearby.

'We untying him?' Saul asked, hurrying ahead to open the door of the weathered old structure.

'No, just shake off the rope—we'll leave his hands tied. I don't figure he can get out of there, but we ain't taking no chances.'

Royce considered the shed, much like the half dozen others scattered about the place. The walls and roof were of aging, warped planks with many cracks and knot holes. The door was of similar material, with the boards held together with crosspieces. It could easily be kicked open, assuming a peg was wedged into the leather-and-staple hasp that now held it shut. If a drop bar was placed in the brackets on either side of it, however, it would be a different matter.

'Hold on a second there, Mister Killer,'

Dallas said, drawing to a halt in front of the shed. Pointing to a low hill on beyond them where the family graveyard, shaded by one of the several cottonwood trees growing on the grounds, had been established, he added: 'Just want to show you where you're going to get planted. Nobody'll ever figure on you being in there—if somebody does come hunting for you.'

'They will,' Royce said flatly.

But such was unlikely, he was certain. There was no one interested enough in his welfare to wonder what had happened to him, unless you thought of Della Harper—and his absence would raise no alarm in her. As far as she knew, he had gone to Texas for an indefinite stay.

'I misdoubt that,' Dallas said, and shoved Jake roughly toward the door. 'Get in there!'

Royce, cursing, stumbled into the shadowy interior of the shed, came up hard against its back wall. The place darkened considerably as one of the Yarbros closed the door. Jake, taut, stood motionless, listening, hoping the wooden bar he'd noticed leaning against the side of the shack would be ignored, that only the hasp would be used to secure the door. His hopes were in vain; shortly he heard the thud of the crossbar being dropped into its brackets. Opening the door from the inside, even if he had the use of his hands, would be difficult.

Royce leaned back, swiped at the sweat on

his forehead, and considered his situation. That the Yarbros would go through with their plans to lynch him—*like the law would*—for shooting Nellie was a foregone conclusion. And he was beyond all possible help from anyone; what was to be done toward freeing him before Will returned with Nellie's body, would have to be done by himself.

Pulling away from the wall, Jake began to prowl the small eight-foot-square room, searching for something that he might use as a tool. Apparently the shed had once been used to stable a cow, or perhaps a horse, as the remainder of what looked to have been a manger had been built against one of the sides. Royce guessed he might dig under one of the walls—they probably were buried no deeper than six or eight inches in the dry ground—if he had something to dig with. It would take something strong, he realized; the soil was as hard as sun-baked clay could get.

There was nothing. The floor of the shed was bare, and there was no way to get his fingers on the edge of a board in the walls and rip off a strip. Such would serve no purpose, anyway; the rocklike ground would quickly reduce it to splinters. He would have to think of something else.

Now again aware of his throbbing hand and aching head—forgotten upon arriving at the Yarbro place—Royce once more probed the interior of the shack for a tool of sorts, for an idea, for any answer to his problem.

His eyes halted on the square-cornered head of a large nail standing an inch or so away from the thick post into which it had been driven. Immediately he crossed to it and with a thumb and forefinger examined the bit of rusting iron. The edges of the head were fairly sharp.

Jake grinned bleakly, stepped to the wall facing the house, and peered through a crack. There was no sign of the Yarbros. All were inside, he reckoned. Wheeling quickly, he dropped to his knees in front of the post, which had been one end of the manger, and began to saw at the nail head with the cord that bound his wrists.

It was slow, tedious work during which he kept an ear cocked for any sounds of the Yarbros stirring about or approaching. This was his one chance and he dare not let it slip away but he was undisturbed, and by the end of the first hour, he was pleased to see that his labor had not gone for nothing; the rawhide was fraying.

Shortly after that he heard the rattle of a wagon and, again seeking out a convenient crack, threw his glance up the rutted road leading into the ranch. It was Will, as he expected, returning with the body of Nellie. Immediately Royce resumed work on the cord; time was running out for him, and it was foolish to waste even a moment watching the

Yarbros.

The heat was intense within the old shack and was made bearable only by the countless cracks and knotholes that admitted air. Jake was soaked with sweat, and occasionally it was necessary to pause and wipe away the drops that gathered on his forehead and misted his eyes.

Arms aching, he drew back from the post for a minute's rest, and hearing sounds in the yard, took advantage of the break to have a look. Only Dallas and Will were in sight. Nellie had been taken from the wagon and carried inside, where she was probably being prepared for burial. Seeing movement on beyond the two men in the direction of the barn, Royce hesitated as he started to turn away. It was Saul, the youngest brother, carrying a coffin that had been hammered together earlier that day.

They would take the elongated pine box inside, lay the blanket-wrapped body of Nellie in it, and nail it shut. Perhaps they would hold a simple service then—or they could wait until they lowered the girl into her grave.

At any rate, the moment was not far off when they'd be coming for him. Pivoting, Jake knelt again at the post and, urgency pressing him, resumed his work on the stubborn rawhide cord.

A short time later the sound of hammering, coming from the Yarbro house, reached him.

CHAPTER THIRTEEN

Jake Royce labored steadily for several minutes and then drew back to examine the rawhide. A bit of satisfaction rolled through him. The cord was now badly frayed. Brushing at the sweat in his eyes, he turned again to the nail. Scarcely had he begun sawing when he heard a noise in the yard. Turning hurriedly to the crack in the opposite wall, he looked out.

The three Yarbro boys—Dallas in the front, Will and Saul at either side and carrying the coffin between them—were approaching, with Ma Yarbro bringing up the rear. Eyes straight ahead, she was a rigid, unforgiving figure in the strong sunlight. They would pass near him, Jake realized, enroute to the burial place on the slope beyond the shed.

Royce moved to the front wall, watched through a knothole as the small cortege marched solemnly by, and then, fearing he might be heard in his efforts to escape, he shifted again, returning to the north wall of the shack where he could see the Yarbros when they reached the grave site.

But he was less interested in the procedure there, once he felt it was safe to resume his work, than he was in wearing through the rawhide binding his wrists, so, hunkering over the post, arms working swiftly, he began sawing away once more at the nail.

He was in a position, nevertheless, to watch, as he was facing in that direction. He saw the procession reach the cemetery and halt. Carefully the brothers placed the coin on two short pieces of timber that had been laid crosswise over the grave, and then, heads bared, stepped back. Ma Yarbro circled by them, took up a stand at the head of the grave. For a long minute she stared at the pine box and then raised her eyes heavenward.

'Lord, this here's my daughter, Nellie, we're sending you. Maybe she was a mite headstrong and wild, but she was a good girl anyway, and I reckon she'd never done any of them bad things folks said she'd done if that no-account Luke Archer hadn't come along.'

Royce, arms straining against the rawhide as he sawed at it, jerked suddenly when the last frayed strands parted. Relief shot through him and he came to his feet quickly. At least there was a chance now that he could get out of the shed and reach his horse, only a few strides away.

'But that ain't nothing you ought to hold against her, Lord. It weren't your fault no more'n it was hers. He was a fast talker, and she was just a youngun that didn't know nothing about his kind. Was my fault, Lord, for not taking better care of her.'

Royce, the droning voice of Ma Yarbro in

94

his ears, shed the remaining strips of cord that dangled from his wrists and dug into a pocket for his folding knife, available to him now that his wrists had been separated. The blade was short, but he was certain it would be long enough to slip between the door and its frame and raise one end of the drop bar out of its bracket.

'Me and her pa had big hopes that Nellie'd find a good man and marry up with him and give us some fine grandchildren. But nothing worked out the way we wanted, Lord. Pa went and died of the flux and the drought just about wiped us out and then Nellie got herself mixed up with that Luke Archer.'

Jake Royce pressed close to the door and, knife blade in the narrow space between crude panel and its frame, lifted upward. The length of wood serving as a crossbar came up readily.

'I'm a thanking you, Lord, for my boys. They're all good and mind what I tell them, and there ain't none of them taken up the devil's ways. And I'm thanking you for that, too—for keeping them out of the hands of painted women and away from demon rum—'

The bar was free of its bracket. Royce, careful not to displace it too far lest it fall and the resulting thud draw attention, pushed the door open a few inches and, reaching through, grasped the length of wood. Holding it tight, Jake raised it out of the other bracket and brought it into the shed.

'Ain't nothing more I got to say, Lord. I'm just hoping you take kindly to Nellie and not send her down into hell's fire. I'll sure be much obliged if you'll sort of overlook her failings and let her have a chair up there with you. We ain't regular churchgoing folks, but we—'

Royce slipped through the door and, closing it quietly, replaced the dropbar. If he could manage to get to his horse, ride off without the Yarbros seeing him, they just might think him still a prisoner in the shed for hours to come since the bar would be in its brackets and appear undisturbed—and a few miles lead on Dallas and his brothers would be a big help.

Bent low, he quickly rounded the corner of the shed, and placing it between himself and the Yarbro family, still grouped about Nellie's grave, he hurried to his horse. A dog, lying in the shade at the side of the house, raised his head and watched indifferently as Royce jerked the reins free of the hitch rack. Still careful to keep the shed, and then house, blocking any view of him by the Yarbros, he led the gelding around the corral and, halting there briefly, swung up onto the saddle.

They had his guns. That thought came to Jake as he settled himself on the black. The Yarbros had taken not only his belt, holster, and pistol, but his rifle as well. They would be in the house, probably on a table or chair near the door—but he'd be a damn fool to try and recover them.

He'd make do with the spare forty-five he'd put in his saddlebags. Twisting about, the cracked voice of Ma Yarbro coming faintly to him through the hot, still air as she continued her supplications, Royce dug the pistol out of the leather pouch and thrust it under his belt as he rode on.

He gained the yard, keeping in the waist-high rabbitbush and stringy sunflowers as much as possible. It was a long eight or ten miles to the main road, and while there might be some advantage to angling across country to reach it, he felt better time could be made on the cleared trail the Yarbros had cut through the ragged growth.

Abruptly a yell echoed through the afternoon's hush. Jake, at the point of congratulating himself on a clean escape, threw a hasty glance over his shoulder. Dallas Yarbro was standing in front of the shed, the door of which was standing open. Ma, with Saul and Will, was hurrying toward him.

'Damn!' Royce swore in exasperation.

He had hoped to be much farther along before his absence was discovered; now he'd have to make a run for it. Even as he cast another quick look at the Yarbros, Dallas broke away from the others and was running to get his horse.

Jake Royce delayed no longer. Raking the big gelding with spurs, he put the horse into a fast gallop. Once he had gained the main road, it would be easier going for the black, since it was less rutted and had fewer weeds. He doubted Dallas Yarbro had a horse that could keep pace with, much less overtake, the black.

He rode on, seeing no more of Yarbro for the next hour or so as the afternoon waned. He was hoping the man would turn back, as he had no desire to kill him—which was what it would come down to if, by some chance, Dallas did catch up. He couldn't help but feel a bit sorry for Ma Yarbro, who had taken the loss of her daughter so bitterly, and he didn't want to deal her any more grief.

They had all been wrong in trying to avenge the girl's death by lynching him. He had only been doing his job when he'd shot the girl, but that contention had failed to stir even the smallest bit of understanding on the part of Ma and her sons.

He had killed Nellie, and regardless of her being an outlaw and undeniably guilty, and he a lawman performing his duty, they had chosen to look at it otherwise and schemed to bring him to account for his actions. There was no doubt in Jake's mind that the Yarbros would have hanged him. Never in his years had he seen such hate in a person's eyes as he'd beheld in those of Ma Yarbro when her sons had brought him in.

Royce shifted in the saddle, allowed the black to slow. He was approaching the sun-blistered and seared area known commonly as

98

the Devil's Kitchen because of the endless piles of flat rocks that daily absorbed enough heat, many claimed, to fry meat on.

He'd avoid the badlands, he decided, follow the example of travelers who knew the country and swing south to the town of Yankee. From there he could connect with another road that bore east to Texas.

Impatiently rubbing the side of his head, still aching dully from the blows he'd taken from the Yarbros, Jake again glanced over his shoulder—and swore. A rider had come into view, one who, odds were, was Dallas Yarbro. It could be someone else, of course, but it looked to be him. He'd best assume it was; he'd be a fool not to.

Abruptly Jake Royce spat. The hell with it! Let Yarbro come. He didn't want more trouble with the family, but he wasn't about to run like a scared rabbit just to avoid it.

He raised his eyes, stared ahead. The turnoff to Yankee had appeared. It would be good to reach the town, sign in at a hotel, and get a night's rest. The previous one had been hectic, and he never had been able to settle down and sleep while he was at Della Harper's. And then, to make matters worse, after starting for Texas he'd run into the Yarbros, which had further tried his patience as well as given him some lumps.

It was a bit cooler moving through the brush- and tree-studded section of the low

99

hills—far better than if he'd kept to the main route that continued on eastward. A thought came to him, and pausing on a slight rise, he looked back over the way he had come.

There was no sign of Dallas—again assuming that was the identity of the rider. And it most likely was, Jake thought. Dallas knew that he was heading for Texas, having heard him mention it; and with that in mind he had kept to the road leading there in the belief that Royce was still somewhere ahead of him.

Jake grinned, brushed at the sweat on his forehead, and moved on. That was good; he could forget about the Yarbros now—and as for Dallas, he was in for a hot time of it in the Devil's Kitchen. The heat at that hour of the day would be well over a hundred degrees.

CHAPTER FOURTEEN

Jake Royce rode into Yankee shortly before sundown. It had been a year or two since he had been there, and then only for an overnight stay; but he could see little change in the settlement.

The Mexican Hat Saloon, with its adjoining hotel, still appeared to be the largest establishment of its kind and enjoying the greatest amount of business. Horton's Livery Stable, Bannerman's Mercantile, the Top Notch Restaurant, and the dozen or so other business firms were as he remembered, except all looked older and more weathered.

The only variation that Jake noticed was the town marshal's office and jail. It had been moved from a building near Bannerman's, was now housed in a new and larger structure built on down the street a short distance.

Wondering who the lawman in charge might be, and ignoring the stares accorded him by persons along the board sidewalk, Royce rode down the center of the street until he reached the hotel. He circled the one-floor, false-fronted building to the stable at its rear. There, after giving the hostler instructions for the care and feeding of the black, and slinging his saddlebags over his shoulder, he returned to the hostelry, entering by its back door.

The clerk was a stranger to him, and he registered without comment, retired to his room long enough to leave the saddlebags and wash up, and then sought out the saloon next door.

The place—noisy, smoke clouds hanging in drifts near the ceiling, heavy with odors—was somewhat crowded, as the night's activities were already well underway. Royce, shouldering his way into a place at the bar, nodded to one of the aproned men behind it.

'Rye whiskey—'

The bartender reached for a bottle and a shot glass, filled the thick-bottomed container to the rim, and slid it across the counter.

'Be a quarter.'

Royce paid, and taking up the glass of liquor said, 'Who's town marshal here?'

The bartender hesitated, looked closely at Jake, and then said, 'Name's Smith—Malachi Smith. You looking for the law?'

'No, was just wondering who was wearing the star. You tell me how to get to Kiowa Springs from here?'

'Sure. Head east out of town. Once you cross the Texas line, bear south on the first road you come to. It'll take you there.'

'Obliged,' Royce said, and, draining his glass, signaled for a refill.

Again paying, and once more tossing off the whiskey in a single gulp, Jake pivoted, hooked his elbows on the edge of the bar, and looked out over the room. The volume of patrons was increasing steadily, and there was a continuous din of voices engaged in conversation punctuated by laughter.

It came to Jake Royce as he stood there that despite all his years he had no real friends. Acquaintances, yes, but no close friends. He'd never actually cultivated any, he supposed; he had always been too busy, too intent on doing his job to get near anyone, take them into his confidence.

Maybe that was a mistake. He wasn't really sure, but he recalled now and then getting a pang of regret that there were no men with whom he could sit down and chew the rag about things in general likc he saw others doing.

What the hell—he wasn't cut out to be a backslapper and a good-time Charlie! He was cut out to be a lawman, and that's all he was—and a damn good one regardless of what a lot of folks thought—and he reckoned he'd go right on to the end of his life being the way he was.

Only—he was no longer a lawman, Jake realized. His star had been taken from him, and by agreeing to take on the job of killing a stranger named Monte Jackson, he had become a hired gun. Royce mulled that fact about in his head, again found it evoked no particular feeling, and dismissed it from his mind. If such was to be his future, so be it; he'd done his damndest to be a good lawman—and evidently failed.

Sighing deeply, Jake turned back to the bartender. Weariness, hunger, and now a strange sort of heaviness were beginning to overtake him.

'Any chance of getting a bit of grub?'

The man nodded. 'We serve regular meals. Today we got steak and potatoes and all the trimmings.'

'Sounds good,' Royce said, reaching for the bottle of whiskey and his glass. 'I'll take the rye along and be over there at one of them back tables. Settle up with you when I'm done.'

He'd little more than sat down and had himself a third drink when the meal, apparently already prepared and awaiting customers, was brought to him by one of the saloon girls who had evidently taken it upon herself to act as his waitress.

'Name's Prissy,' she said as she placed the platter of food before him. 'You want some company?'

Royce favored the woman with a slanting glance. Probably in her mid-twenties, he guessed. She had light, honey-colored hair, brown eyes, a good, full figure, and a happy smile. Her dress, knee length and cut low at the neck to reveal her arching breasts, was a bright red and trimmed with ivory-colored lace that was somewhat soiled. A bit of cheerful companionship might be just what be needed to get him out of the mood he was in, Jake decided.

'Sure. Get yourself a glass—and order up a meal if you're hungry.'

'A drink'll be fine,' Prissy said. 'I've already had supper—things start early around here,' she added, and crossed to the bar.

Returning with a shot glass, she sat down, filled it from the bottle, and then, holding it between a thumb and forefinger, considered him thoughtfully.

'Mind telling me your name?'

Royce paused, a forkful of gravy-drenched mashed potatoes on the way to his mouth. 'Jake.'

She repeated the word. 'That's all?'

'That's all,' he replied.

Prissy smiled, took a sip of her whiskey. 'I side with you—last names sure ain't needful. I don't recollect seeing you around here before.'

'Been a spell since I was. Was just riding through then—same as I am now.'

'Heading south for Mexico, I reckon—'

'Texas—'

Prissy laughed. 'Ain't much difference.' Then, 'You running from the law?'

Jake hesitated again, laid down his fork. Had that much of a change come over him? Folks used to say he looked like a lawman—now here was a girl who pegged him for an outlaw dodging the law!

'Nope,' he said, and resumed eating.

But the thought tugged at his mind. Maybe he actually was an outlaw in reality, needing only to perform the task he was being paid to do to make it absolute. And maybe he had been an outlaw all along, had simply not been considered as such because of the star he wore.

That was wrong—all wrong. He had been doing his job, Jake reassured himself doggedly—and he sure hadn't been the one who made the rule that the world was to be divided into two camps—those who kept the law and those who broke it. That was the way it was before he came along, and he was pretty sure that's how it would be long after he'd been planted in some dusty boneyard somewhere.

In his own judgment, he had done no unnecessary killing, regardless of what a lot of folks thought, had used his pistol only when forced to. And when you came right down to brass nails, even if there had been a couple of times when he maybe could have held off a bit before going for his gun, or even avoiding such, wasn't the country better off with another renegade out of the way and not left to roam the streets and trails?

'You sure do take your eating serious—'

At Prissy's comment, Jake leaned back in his chair, and relinquished his knife and fork. The plate wasn't clean, but he'd had all he wanted.

106

'Was thinking about something else—'

Prissy smiled. 'I'm a pretty good listener if you're of mind to talk about it.'

Royce considered that, recalling as he did the ideas he'd once heard a gambler, well into his cups and consequently overflowing with sage advice, detail to a handful of listeners on the subject of women. *God made them soft and warm, and sometimes beautiful, so that a man would have pleasant thoughts to hang onto while he was going through hell*, he'd said. And Jake had let it go, more or less, at that. He'd never devoted much time to discussing anything of note with any woman—and had seen no reason to change. Perhaps, he thought now, he'd been wrong there, too!

'Hashing over a couple of things about the law and outlaws,' he said, taking up his drink. 'Been wondering if just shooting them down, killing them, wasn't the best way to civilize the country and make it safe for decent folks to live in.'

Prissy frowned, pressed her full, red lips together. 'I reckon it could be,' she said, finally. 'Only it seems to me a thing like that could sure get out of hand.'

'Meaning?'

'Well, there's all kinds of outlaws, some real bad ones—killers—and they ought to die. And then there's the penny-ante kind who ain't nothing but two-bit grifters who never hurt nobody much.'

'They're all outlaws—breaking the law—'

'Sure, but what I'm thinking is that them who decide which ones are to die and which ones are to live could turn out to be the worst outlaws of any—having all that say-so.'

'When a man pins on a star, he swears to treat everybody square and equal—'

'I suppose that's true most times, but it ain't always so,' Prissy replied, glancing toward the far corner of the room where the piano player, accompanied by a black man with a banjo, had struck up a lively tune. Couples were rising from their tables and drifting over from the bar to gather in the roped-off area reserved for dancing.

The girl brought her attention back to Royce, who at that moment was in the process of removing the bandage from his injured hand.

'Seen that you got hurt,' she said. 'It sore?'

Royce tossed the dust-stained bandage into a nearby cuspidor and flexed his fingers. He'd noticed but little pain since around mid-afternoon, reckoned Della Harper's remedy had done its job.

'Was, ain't now,' he said, continuing to exercise the digits as well as the wrist.

'Was wondering,' the girl said then, looking again to the shuffling couples, 'if you wanted to dance.'

Royce grinned, shook his head. 'Not exactly what I was figuring on. You got a room around

108

here?'

Prissy returned his smile. 'In back—a real private one.'

'Let's go,' Jake said, and grasping the whiskey bottle by the neck with one hand and the two glasses with the other, he shoved back his chair and got to his feet.

Prissy rose quickly, hurriedly moved out in front of him to lead the way, but immediately to her left a heavyset man came upright, blocking her. The girl halted and fell back a step in alarm, but the man's hard glance was not on her but upon Jake Royce.

'Hold it, Marshal,' he ordered in a challenging tone of voice.

CHAPTER FIFTEEN

Royce eased back, settled himself squarely on his booted feet, and stared at the man. Squat, with coal black hair, full mustache and beard, he had small, agatelike eyes. His lips were drawn back, exposing broad, tobacco-stained teeth, and there was about him—slightly crouched and big shoulders thrown forward—a definite hostility.

'Not a marshal,' Royce said. 'No more.'

'But you was. I been setting here looking at you. Weren't sure it was you till you got up, seen then it was.'

Jake continued to study the man as he probed his mind for a clue to the fellow's identity. Other saloon patrons close by had suspended whatever they were engaged in doing and turned their attention to the two men, now facing each other at little more than an arm's length. Elsewhere in the crowded room, matters were as they had been; the click of cards, chink of coins, the rumbling of voices and scraping of heels on the board floor filling the hot, motionless air. The dancing had ceased as the music ended, and over near that roped-off area there was the sound of breaking glass as something fragile was dropped, followed by a peal of laughter as a woman found humor in the incident.

'Ain't you recollecting me, Marshal?'

Royce shook his head. A face out of the past—an outlaw, probably, to judge from the man's attitude.

'Can't say as I do.'

'Well, you sure as hell ought! I'm Boomer Wickam. You sent me to the pen for five years—and you killed my partner.'

The name unlocked Jake's memory. There had been a holdup—a bank. He had encountered the robbers as they came from the building and were hurrying to reach their horses. Both men had weapons in their hands and had opened fire when they saw him approaching. He had brought his own weapon into play then, wounding Wickam and killing the man with him.

'I'm remembering,' Royce murmured.

A tautness had come over him, sharpening his senses, placing him on guard. It was forever this way, he thought; an outlaw apprehended, found guilty, and sent to the penitentiary always returned, after serving his time, with vengeance in his heart. None could ever admit to himself that he deserved the sentence meted out to him by the judge, only blamed the lawman instrumental in bringing him to justice.

Wickam's eyes were upon the pistol thrust under Royce's waist band. He had intended to buy himself a belt and holster to replace the one taken by the Yarbros, while he was in

Yankee, but as yet he had not found the opportunity.

'You're a' wearing your iron mighty handy these days, Marshal,' Boomer said, and then added, 'Now don't you go worrying none about me carrying a grudge against you.'

Jake's shoulders stirred indifferently. He half turned, handed the bottle of whiskey and glasses to Prissy as a hard smile cracked his lips. He had learned long since that the words that came out of a man's mouth—especially that of an outlaw—didn't necessarily reveal his true intentions.

'Wouldn't be anything new,' Royce said softly.

'Well, I ain't saying I am and I ain't saying I'm not,' Wickam said evasively. 'I sure reckon ought—you sending me up and causing me to lose my woman. And that partner of mine you blew to hell—Ernie Barr, I reckon I owe you for him, too. He had a family, a wife and four younguns. You know what become of them?'

The group encircling Royce and Boomer Wickam had increased twofold as more of the Mexican Hat's patrons, suddenly aware of the gathering near the bar and sensing excitement, hurried to become a part of it.

Jake made no reply to the question. Boomer glanced about, a look of scorn on his dark features.

'Folks,' he said loudly, 'this here jasper is, or maybe I best say was, one of them real mean

112

badge toters, the kind that thinks they're the right hand of God or something like that and can do any damn thing they want.'

A murmur of disapproval drifted through the saloon. Somewhere in the crowd a man growled: *the lousy sonofabitch.* At that, one of the men behind the bar, the saloon's proprietor apparently, fearing the worst, climbed up onto a chair where he could be seen by all.

'I don't want no trouble in here!' he shouted. 'All of you folks just back off and go on about what you were doing. And Boomer— you and your friend there go on outside and do your fighting. I don't want my place busted up!'

Wickam seemed not to hear. 'Them little kids I was telling you about,' he began, taking up the tale of his partner's family, 'they got sick and died. The woman, too. Folks said they just starved to death.'

'You can't blame that on the marshal,' said a well-dressed man leaning against the bar. 'You want to blame somebody other'n this partner you're talking about, blame the family's neighbors. If they were decent people, they'd stepped in and—'

'They was living in a tar-paper shack out on the flats about ten mile from town. Didn't have no neighbors.'

'They sound like squatters to me,' the well-dressed man observed, dryly. 'Start out with

113

nothing and most always end up with nothing. You can't expect much—'

'I ain't talking about that!' Wickam cut in angrily. 'I'm saying if the marshal there hadn't been in such an all-fired hurry to use his gun, Ernie would be alive today—same as his family would.'

A brief hush followed that, and then a squat, beefy man in a dusty brown suit and collarless shirt said, 'How do you figure that, Boomer? Your partner might've been alive, but he'd've been in the pen, same as you. And far as his family was concerned, he couldn't help them none.'

Wickam nodded. 'Yeh, but they would've known he was alive and took heart from that 'cause they'd be figuring he'd come home when his time was up.'

'Well, that kind of figuring sure can't be put in a pot and cooked,' someone commented.

'For sure!' another voice chimed in. 'I'm wondering about that woman. Appears to me she could've got work somewheres and made a little something so's she could feed her youngsters.'

'Maybe so—but you all are overlooking what Boomer's getting at,' a slim, red-faced man declared. 'He's saying this jasper was too handy with his shooting iron, and I'm believing him. He didn't kill Boomer—why'd he have to kill Boomer's partner? Why couldn't he have just arrested him, too?'

Again a threatening mutter traveled through the crowd. It died off when still another voice said, 'You want to tell us why, Marshal?'

Royce, simmering beneath his calm exterior, eyes pulled down to little more than slits, stared at the speaker for a long breath and then shook his head.

'I don't have to explain what I do to anybody—'

'The hell you don't! Wearing a star don't give a man the right to murder!'

'Wasn't murder,' Jake said, flatly. 'Fact is I've never murdered a man in my life—shot it out with a few, like I did with Ernie Barr. I'll admit that, but every man I've shot down was trying to kill me.'

'Oh, sure—was what them fancy lawyers calls self-defense.'

'Can call it what you like, but when a man shoots at me, I sure'n hell aim to shoot back,' Royce said quietly. 'It's either kill or be killed at a time like that, and I don't much favor the last idea.'

'Which still don't change what I been talking about,' Boomer Wickam declared. 'Was him and his high-handed ways—always being right and doing what he damn well pleased— that caused that woman and her kids to die. Way I see that, it ain't nothing but pure murder!'

'That's right! Was no need to kill that there

115

partner of Boomer's. And if he hadn't, them kids and that woman'd be alive right now, likely!'

'How about that, Marshal? Ain't that so?'

Royce, tall shape rigid in the smoky light of the saloon, arms folded across his chest, smiled faintly. Turning his head slightly to see the girl, Prissy, the smile faded. She had set the bottle of rye and the two glasses they were using on a nearby table and disappeared, deciding apparently that she wanted nothing to do with a man who had brought about the death of a woman and her helpless children. The smile returned at that point, but this time it was a hard, brittle expression of contempt. It wasn't the first time he'd experienced the loneliness of being hated—and likely it would not be the last.

'No—it sure as hell ain't!' he snapped, anger now beginning to get the best of him. There was still no indication of such in his manner, however, except a bunching of hard lines at the corners of his mouth.

'Boomer and Barr were robbing a bank. When they came out, they came shooting. I stopped them the only way I could. Barr got a bullet in the heart, Boomer took one in the leg. If he claims it was any different, he's a damn liar.'

The hush that gripped the saloon became even deeper, more tense. Royce lowered his arms gently, allowed his hands to hang at his

116

sides. Wickam, legs spread, head forward, arms also down, glanced about as if assuring himself of support from the crowd, now edging away as they sought to remove themselves from the line of fire. Finally, sweat shining on his dark skin, Boomer swore.

'I ain't taking that from nobody,' he began, and broke off suddenly as the crowd parted, formed a short aisle to admit the lean figure of a man wearing a star.

'Be enough of that kind of talk, Boomer,' he said in a sharp, uncompromising tone, as he drew to a halt.

CHAPTER SIXTEEN

'Now, I want to know what's going on here?'

The lawman—dressed in a gray suit, a white shirt with string tie, a high-crowned, wide-brimmed range hat, and wearing cross-belted pistols—glanced about. He had a stern, narrow face accented by a black mustache and beard, and his thick brows were like a dark shelf over his pale blue eyes. It was clear from the respect being accorded him that he brooked no nonsense.

'Come on, Boomer—I want to hear it!'

Wickam, his coiled shape relenting, grinned. 'Just come across a old friend, Marshal. Was saying howdy.'

'That ain't likely,' the lawman said, shaking his head. 'Any fool can see there's more going on than that.'

He paused, looked about as if expecting someone in the crowd to speak up, give him an explanation, but no one did. The old unwritten but well-understood rule observed by witnesses in general—say nothing and thereby not get involved—was holding true, Royce saw.

Such had always been a source of irritation to him. Bystanders could make a lawman's job much simpler and easier if they would talk, reveal what they knew, but it was seldom one did. The reason was obvious; too many times the parties concerned would seek out the person who had spoken up and exact vengeance upon him for his cooperation.

'Was just what I was doing, Marshal,' Wickam insisted. 'You ain't got no right to go jumping me when I ain't—'

'You better remember what I told you,' the lawman—Malachi Smith, the bartender had said his name was—warned briskly. 'Start trouble in my town and I'll boot you out! I ain't wanting you here in the first place, but I've got no ground to run you out unless you break the law. Now, I'm watching you close— and if you step out of line just one time, that'll be the end of it.'

'Hell, Marshal, I ain't—'

'Best thing you can do is clear out of here, go some place else—right now!' the lawman snapped. 'I just might change my mind about overlooking this!'

Boomer Wickam stared defiantly at the marshal for a brief moment, then shrugging, wheeled and cut back through the crowd to the doorway. He paused there, glanced over his shoulder at Royce, and then passed on through the wide entrance into the night.

'Now who're you?'

Royce, eyes never leaving Wickam until the onetime outlaw had disappeared from view, heard the marshal's hard-edged question and brought his attention back to the slender man standing before him.

'Name's Jake Royce.'

'I'm Smith—Malachi Smith. I'm the marshal here, I reckon you can see that if you ain't blind.'

Royce had turned, was retrieving his bottle of whiskey and one of the glasses. Nearby, Malachi Smith's expression was altering.

'Seems I've heard of you,' he said coldly. 'A lawman—a town marshal, I think it was. Somewhere north of here.'

'Parsonville—but I'm not the marshal there any more.'

Smith nodded slowly. 'From what I've been told, I expect the town's better off.'

Temper again rose within Jake Royce. Smith had evidently heard some of the rumors floating around the Territory about him. Being a fellow lawman, however, you'd think he'd understand such things and know that tales of that nature were generally started by some outlaw complaining that he'd not been treated right. But, let it ride. It didn't matter—not any more.

'Could be,' he drawled.

'What do you want around here? If you ain't wearing a badge no more, you ain't got no business coming here looking for—'

'I'm no bounty hunter—I'm not looking for anybody,' Royce said. 'Just riding through.'

'Which way?'

'Can't see as that's any business of yours,

Marshal, but I'm not hiding anything. I'm heading east—for Texas.'

The crowd that had pulled away when violence between Royce and Boomer Wickam appeared imminent had closed in again, and all present were listening closely to what was being said.

'You got a lawing job over there?'

'Don't figure that's any of your business, either, but the answer is no, I don't.'

Smith, the front of his coat swept back to better display his cross-belted guns, allowed the garment to fall back into place. He glanced about, seemingly in deep thought, and Jake wondered what might be going through the lawman's mind. He was realizing, too, that the tenor of the crowd had changed drastically since his identity had been revealed; where it had been more or less divided in its attitude toward him, it was now definitely for Boomer.

'You running him out of town, Marshal?' a man standing at the bar asked.

'Sure ought,' a voice somewhere in the crowd observed. 'We plain don't want no killer hanging around here.'

Malachi Smith raised a hand for silence while he gave the idea thought. Finally, 'I ain't decided yet. The man ain't busted no law.'

'But we all know what he is—a killer marshal—'

'Just knowing he done something don't cut no hay—it's seeing him do something wrong

121

that counts. There's a big difference.' Smith switched his hard eyes back to Royce. 'How long you figuring to hang around?'

'Told you I was riding through. Aim to pull out in the morning right after I have a bite to eat and buy myself a new holster and belt outfit.'

Smith now gave that thought. Then, 'Did I have my druthers, I've have you riding on right now, but I reckon I can't keep you from doing your sleeping here tonight. Your kind means nothing but bad trouble, and I sure as hell want you gone first-off in the morning.'

'Then I take it you're agreeable to me staying over—'

Smith wagged his head and swore. 'Damn it, can't you savvy plain English? Can stay long as you keep your nose clean—just don't be here by the time the sun's hot tomorrow morning.'

The crowd, now that there was no doubt that all possibility of excitement was over, had begun to break up, some members drifting back to their table or to the bar while others resumed gambling. The piano player and his banjo accompanist struck up a tune, and shortly the dance floor was again filled with stomping swaying couples.

'I'd as soon you'd get out of here—take your bottle and get a room in the hotel,' Jake heard the lawman say.

He shrugged, grinned. 'What I had in mind, Marshal. I'm not looking for trouble any more than you not wanting me to find any.'

'Mighty glad to hear you say that,' Smith said, and setting his wide-brimmed hat more firmly on his head, he wheeled and started for the doorway.

Royce, a half smile on his lips, watched the lawman depart. There was an arrogance to the man, likely adopted to offset his somewhat slight stature. But Jake was not underestimating the man's ability and effectiveness; the two pistols he carried and evidently knew well how to use were equalizers that put him on a level with any and all.

CHAPTER SEVENTEEN

It occurred to Jake Royce as he rode out of Yankee that next morning a time after sunrise that he had seen nothing of Dallas Yarbro while in the settlement. He thus came to the final conclusion that, as suspected, he'd thrown the man off his trail that previous day.

Jake was pleased it had turned out that way—and that puzzled him a bit, gave him food for thought. Ordinarily he could have cared less whether Yarbro had overtaken him and attempted a shootout. Like as not he would have even halted and allowed the man to catch up—but he hadn't. Were the loss of his star and the demonstrations of hatred that had surfaced since getting to him?

Hell, he thought, shaking his head. It couldn't be—and for one big reason: it didn't matter that much to him. And even if it did—what of it? He'd only done his job as he saw it.

Brushing that from his mind, he reached down, let his hand touch the holster now hanging at his hip. It was not a new one, nor was the belt, now filled with gleaming brass cartridges, that he'd purchased from Bannerman just before riding out. The merchant had a stock of new ones, but they were stiff and hard, and it would take weeks to break in the leather properly—and Royce was of no mind to bother with that. A worn, well-oiled pocket for his forty-five suited him just fine, and the feel of it—gently rocking against his leg—was comforting.

Settling himself into the saddle, he allowed the black to ease along at a slow lope. It was cool and pleasant at that hour of the day, with the sky to the east still showing bits of color left over from sunrise, and the purple-tasseled grass glistening with dew as a faint breeze stirred about.

Robber jays were fluttering in the cedars and brush, and over on a rail fence well off the road, meadowlarks were whistling. He wished the entire route to Texas could be as pleasant as this that lay close to the town, but he knew that it would change shortly. Then he would be faced with skirting the lower end of Devil's Kitchen for a considerable distance. That much he knew of the area; once across the line and in Texas, moving south for Kiowa Springs, he had no idea of the nature of the country he'd be traveling.

A flash of alarm shot through Jake Royce. It was purely intuitive, for he had seen nothing and heard nothing, yet the subconscious warning was there—as positive and tangible as a road sign.

He gave no indication that he sensed anything wrong, simply remained motionless on his saddle and let the black continue at his easy pace. But his glance, sharp and relentless

125

from beneath hooded eyes, was sweeping back and forth, probing every clump of rabbitbush and Apache plume, each thick-branched cedar as well as all rocks along the trail large enough for concealment. And then in an aislelike clearing in a stand of brush off to his right, Royce saw sudden motion, and an instant later Boomer Wickam stepped out to face him.

Jake swore raggedly. He should have known Boomer would not let it drop there in Yankee, that since they had met and the old scars had been raked open Wickam would seek out an opportunity to square up what he considered a wrong.

'Far as you're going, Marshal,' the outlaw called as Royce pulled the black to a sliding halt.

His hand was resting on the butt of the pistol hanging at his side. His legs were apart, his hat pushed back, and shoulders pitched forward, and he was ready to draw and fire.

'Don't try it,' Royce warned, quieting the startled gelding. 'I'll kill you, Boomer—you know that.'

There was no boast in the statement. It was purely a declaration of a cold, brutal fact. Wickam frowned, but his taut, heavyset figure did not relent. Nevertheless, the words had their effect. Boomer had hesitated, and in that fragment of time Jake Royce had gotten his horse under control and was reaching for his own weapon.

126

'You ain't telling me nothing!' Wickam shouted, recovering from his brief lapse and jerking his pistol from its holster.

Royce fired as the outlaw leveled his weapon. Boomer staggered back, a red stain appearing magically on his chest and spreading rapidly. Reflex action caused his finger to tighten on the trigger of his pistol. The gun went off, sending the bullet into the dry, sunbaked ground at his feet as he fell heavily.

'That'll be them—on up a ways!'

The shout came from beyond a screen of brush along the road. Instantly Royce set his spurs to the black and rode the big horse off into the cedars beyond the sprawled figure of Wickam.

A dozen yards away, and well hidden, Jake pulled up and, moving a bit to his left where he could see the dead outlaw, waited, wondering just who it had been that had trailed him, and why.

The answer was not long in coming. In only moments, two men appeared coming out of the brush carefully, pistols drawn. Royce swore softly. One was Malachi Smith; the other, a younger individual also with a star on his vest, was evidently a deputy.

'Looks like he got away,' Smith said, looking around. Then, holstering his pistols, he stepped into the road and moved up to Wickam. Rolling the man to his back, the lawman considered the dusty shape for a breath and said, 'Right through the brisket. Reckon old Boomer never knew what hit him.'

The deputy had followed the marshal into the road, was now hunched over the outlaw. 'Had his gun out, but I reckon he wasn't fast enough for that there fellow.'

Malachi Smith brushed back his tall hat. 'Knew this here's what'd happen and was hoping to be in on it, 'cause all I want is one chance at Royce. There ain't nobody I hate more'n a killer marshal.'

The deputy, taking the pistol from Boomer's stiffening fingers, looked off down the road. 'You figure you can take him, Marshal?'

'Know for sure I can,' Smith said lifting his glance to the road also.

'Well, I'm betting he ain't got far—we was here only a couple of minutes after the shooting.'

Malachi Smith shook his head. 'Sure wish I'd got here in time.'

'Well, let's go after him,' the deputy said, rising and thrusting Wickam's pistol under his belt. 'He's around somewheres close—and there ain't nothing we can do for Boomer. Can track him down—that is, if you're for damn sure you can take him, Marshal.'

The deputy's words ended, seemingly hung in the warm, quiet air. Smith shifted his gaze to the younger man, recognizing the challenge they carried. His hand was being politely

128

called, he knew, and he had no choice but to back up what he had said.

'You're right, Zeke—he can't've got far. Let's get the horses.'

Immediately the deputy wheeled and hurried back up the road to disappear beyond a bend and return shortly with their animals. Smith turned briskly to meet the deputy, took the reins of the bay he was evidently riding, and swung onto the saddle. He nodded to Zeke, who was also mounting.

'He's tricky, this here Royce, so we best go mighty careful. You take the right side of the road, and I'll stay on the left. Keep your eyes peeled, now!'

'Aim to do that for sure!' the deputy declared fervently.

Royce, well back in the brush, watched the pair approach. Despite the seriousness of the situation, a grin was pulling at the corners of his mouth, and there was a flicker of humor in his narrowed, gray eyes.

'Don't let him get behind you,' he heard Marshal Smith warn. 'He ain't a bit bashful about shooting a man in the back.'

'That so?' Zeke said. 'Never figured him for a man who'd—'

'How'd you think he got that reputation of his? Weren't because he hauled in a lot of outlaws, was because he gunned down a lot of them—and then brought them in. And was the truth ever to get out, folks would know that damn near every man he went out to get wound up dead.'

'How many you figure he got that way?'

'Oh, I expect the tally'd come up to twenty, maybe even twenty-five.'

The faint smile faded from Jake Royce's lips. Twenty! Twenty-five! Hell, he no doubt had collared and brought in that number of dangerous outlaws, probably even more during his time as a lawman, but he sure as hell hadn't killed that many men! A dozen, perhaps, but certainly no more than that; and they—every damned one of them—had forced his hand!

'Jeez!' the deputy said in a low, wheezing voice. 'I see now why you feel like you do about him. His kind of man ain't fit to wear a star.'

Smith and Zeke, riding slow, were now directly in front of Royce. From the depths of the dense brush he watched them pass. The humorous aspect of the episode had evaporated and been replaced by a building irritation, and when the two lawmen had gone by and were a dozen or so paces down the road, Jake drew his pistol and, clucking to the gelding, rode out into the open.

'Marshal!' he called harshly. 'Pull up!'

Smith and his deputy came to an abrupt stop. Royce moved in nearer.

'Want you to keep your hands where I can see them,' he directed. 'Heard you telling the deputy there how I'm a great one at back-

130

shooting. Well, you make a wrong move and I just might have to prove it.'

The irritation tightening Royce had faded as quickly as it had come, and a streak of humor was again flowing through Royce.

'What're you aiming to do?' Malachi Smith asked. His voice was a bit high, and there was a hint of fear in it.

'First off, I want you both to drop your guns—means that one you took off Boomer Wickam, too, Deputy. Do it real slow. I sure would hate to make a mistake and kill you just on account of you moving sudden like.'

'Yes, sir,' Zeke replied hurriedly.

'And keep looking right on down the road.'

Again the deputy signified his understanding. The marshal was more deliberate. When the three pistols were laying in the loose dust, Royce holstered his weapon and, folding his arms across his chest, settled back in the saddle.

'Best you get something straight, Marshal. Those were pure lies you were telling the deputy. I've never shot a man in the back in my life—and it's closer to a dozen outlaws that I've had to kill than twenty or twenty-five. Fact is, I've never done anything to shame the star I was wearing.'

'That mean you ain't going to kill us?' Zeke asked in a faltering voice.

Royce smiled crookedly. 'Haven't made up my mind yet, Deputy. Heard the marshal say he'd like to shoot it out with me. Expect that's what I ought to do—accommodate him, let him have his chance.'

Malachi Smith stirred uneasily on his horse. 'Now, Marshal,' he said, 'I—I didn't exactly mean that. What I did mean was that if all the things I'd heard about you were true, then maybe somebody ought to do something about it.'

'And you figure you're the one?'

The lawman shifted again. 'No, I don't reckon I exactly mean that, either—'

Royce laughed. 'Then maybe you best make it plain to the deputy and me so we'll both savvy.'

The marshal's shoulder went down. He shook his head. 'All right,' he said in a frustrated kind of voice. 'I was shooting off my mouth. I ain't about to draw iron against you, Royce. Wouldn't stand a chance, and I damn well know it."

'What about the things you were saying about me?'

'Just what I've heard.'

'And you didn't know whether they were straight talk or lies?'

'No, sure didn't. Only heard—'

'But you went right ahead repeating them same as if you knew for sure they were true?'

'Yeh, guess I did.'

Royce swore. 'Seems to me you're the one bringing shame to a lawman's star. You not only pass along a bunch of rumors about another man, but you make it sound like they're all gospel truth. How long've you been doing that?'

Smith swore raggedly, carefully raised a hand and brushed at the sweat on his face. 'Couple years, maybe. Ain't known of you much longer'n that.'

'A couple of years—a man can do a lot of damage to another man's reputation in a couple of years! And there's always a lot of folks willing to listen to something bad about a lawman—you ought to know that.'

'Yeh, expect so.'

'Way this adds up, I think I ought to do something about it—about you. I'm finding it mighty hard to just let it pass.'

There was a long silence broken only by the clacking of insects in the brush and the restless stamping of the deputy's horse, and then Smith said: 'I admit I got it coming, Royce. I was a dang fool to do any talking when I didn't know what I was saying. Can bet I ain't ever doing anything like that again—not about you or any man. Just what do you figure to do to us—me?'

'Ain't decided yet. Just want you and the deputy to keep looking straight ahead while I figure it out. Understand?'

'Sure do,' Zeke replied as the marshal nodded.

Royce wheeled the black about quietly and,

walking the big horse in the muffling dust, doubled back up the road until he was well out of hearing distance. Then, cutting sharp right, he struck out across country for Texas.

A quarter hour later when he topped out a hill well to the east, he looked over his shoulder. Malachi Smith and his deputy were still waiting, motionless, on their horses for him to announce his decision.

CHAPTER EIGHTEEN

It was late in the day when Jake Royce, dusty, trail worn, and in no good frame of mind, rode into Kiowa Springs. He reined the black gelding, also tired, up to the hitch rack fronting the Great Western Hotel and halted. Not dismounting, he sat motionless, studying the street.

It was a trail driver's town. Jake recognized that fact immediately from the bullet-pocked signs of the few stores, the large number of saloons, and the several houses where carelessly dressed women lounged in the windows and doorways. There was also a scarcity of the usual business houses, there being in evidence only one general merchandise store, a gun shop, a livery stable and saddlery, a barber—with hot water available for bathing—and three or four restaurants.

The general appearance of the settlement was one of neglect and disrepair, which was to be expected in a town where the existence of the merchants depended upon the patronage of drovers and others connected with the trail drives.

Sighing, Royce came off the saddle and settled himself squarely on his feet in the loose dust. He was accustomed to riding, and ordinarily his muscles and bones had no complaint at the end of the day, but the journey from Parsonville had been a long one and he was feeling the effects of every mile traveled.

Pulling off his saddlebags, Jake stepped up onto the porch and entered the hotel, a low-ceilinged, dingy affair with rooms extending off a hallway running back from the small lobby. An elderly man greeted him with no more than a nod, shoved a book and pencil at him across a scarred, makeshift counter.

'Sign up,' he said. 'Room's a dollar.'

Royce entered his name on the smudged page, paid the specified charge, and reached for the key the clerk had set forth.

'Number Seven. End of the hall. Stable your horse out back,' the elderly clerk said, as if by rote, and turned away.

Royce also wheeled, and walking the length of the corridor, located his room. Opening the door, he hung the saddlebags over the back of a chair and, returning to the hall, continued out the rear door to the yard behind the building. Another aging man, looking very much like the hotel's clerk, was sitting in a chair propped against the front wall of the stable.

'You the hostler?'

The bearded oldster rocked forward and came to his feet. 'Reckon I am. You wanting something?'

'Want my horse taken care of. Black gelding out front—'

'I know where he is,' the hostler said. 'Set right here and seen you ride up. What do you want me to do with him?'

'Rub him down, and grain him. It's been a long trip.'

'You be coming for him later?'

'Likely not till morning—but there is a chance I might need him sooner.'

The old man nodded. 'That'll cost you a dollar and a half. Pay my brother there in the hotel. Your horse'll be ready anytime after a hour or so, if you want him.'

Royce returned to his room. During his brief absence the big china pitcher had been filled with water, and two clean, if somewhat worn, towels now hung on the rack at the end of the washstand.

Jake stripped, washed himself down with the tepid water, and then he shook the dust from the clothing he had shed and drew it back on. He hadn't bothered to buy a change and guessed that was one of the first things he'd better do after he'd taken care of Monte Jackson and after McQueen had paid him off.

The bathing had improved his outlook considerably, and now in a much better frame of mind, he trod the length of the Great Western once more and was again on the street.

The black was gone, the hostler having

come for him, and at that moment was likely enjoying a bag of oats while getting a gunnysack rubdown. He was a good animal, seldom faltered even under the most trying conditions, and he deserved the best of care when it was available.

Moving off the hotel's porch, Royce started down the street. There were but few persons abroad at that late afternoon hour, he noted as he let his glance sweep the irregular row of buildings for Dundee's Saloon. He'd given no more thought to Dallas Yarbro since losing him at the turn off to Yankee, and he hoped he'd see no more of him, or of the Boomer Wickams with their grudges, until after he had located the man McQueen wanted dead. They would only complicate matters for him, and he wanted nothing cluttering his mind and interfering with concentration. Once the job was done, he'd be only too pleased to have it out with Yarbro, or anyone else who felt they had a call coming.

Dundee's Saloon . . . His eyes caught sight of the place about halfway down the street. Small, with a narrow front, but boasting an upper floor, it had a weathered, hardused look. Yellowing paper was pasted over its broken windows, and a landing sagged at one end.

Pointing for it, and shaking his head at a woman who had abruptly appeared in one of the two open windows of the second floor and called down to him, Royce stepped up onto the landing, crossed, and elbowing aside the single batwing door that guarded the entrance to the establishment, went inside.

It was dark and quiet. For a brief time Royce stood quiet, allowed his eyes to adjust to the meager light provided by two or three oil lamps, and then, as his vision stabilized, glanced about and located the bar. It was a crude but sturdy affair of thick planks, uprights, and cross pieces, with a single shelf nailed to the wall behind to serve as a backbar. Three men, who were seated at a table near the stairway leading to the second story, and the bartender, were the only persons present in the room.

'You Ernshaw?' Royce asked, motioning for the man to pour him a drink.

The bartender nodded, moved to comply. 'Surprises me aplenty you not asking me if I'm Dundee. Every stranger that comes in here figures I am.'

Jake shrugged, dropped a quarter on the worn surface of the counter, and reached for his drink. Somewhere in the near distance a train whistled in forlorn, lonely tones.

'Don't surprise me none,' he said. 'Name's on the sign.'

'Yeh, I reckon that's it,' Ernshaw admitted. 'Going to have to change that someday.'

'How long's this Dundee been gone?' Royce asked, glancing at the men at the table. The

139

woman he'd seen in the window, accompanied by another wearing a robe of some kind, had come from their rooms and were slowly descending the stairs.

'Couple of years . . . You want something special, asking for me by name, or you just being sociable?'

'I'm looking for Monte Jackson,' Jake replied, jerking a thumb at the three men gathered about the table. 'He one of them over there?'

Ernshaw had come to quick attention. He studied Royce briefly, looked off toward the door and shook his head.

'Nope, he ain't.'

'Was told you could tell me where I can find him—'

The saloonkeeper said, 'Yeh, I reckon I can—but it'll take me a little time. Got to do some asking around. You putting up at the hotel for the night?'

Royce downed his drink. 'Took a room there. Can find me there—Number Seven—after I've had a bite to eat.'

'Getting about that time, all right,' Ernshaw said genially. 'You go right ahead. Soon's I can get Monte Jackson located, I'll send word to you.'

Jake nodded, smiled at the woman hovering close by, and returned to the street.

Darkness was not far off, he noted. The sun was down and shadows along the way were beginning to darken. No lamps were yet visible in any of the stores or most of the saloons, but with the coolness that came with sunset, a few persons were now moving about on the walks. Kiowa Springs would have but few permanent residents; a trail town was no place for a man to raise a family.

The Red Bluff Restaurant—Home Cooking. Royce spotted the cafe's battered sign farther down the street, and since he doubted there would be much difference between their fare and that of their competitors', he decided he would have his evening meal there. Moreover, Dundee's Saloon stood in the intervening distance between it and the Great Western, and he could drop in there on his return walk to the hotel and see if Ernshaw had any word for him.

The meal was hearty and plentiful, and while he had many times in the past enjoyed tastier food, it served its purpose. Topping it all off with a third cup of coffee, he paid his check and retired to the now dark street.

Strolling leisurely along, a stogie selected from the stock at the restaurant between his teeth, Jake made his way to Dundee's. Ernshaw had stepped out on business for a few minutes, one of the women advised him, and in the next breath issued a personal invitation to come upstairs and wait for the saloonman's return. Royce smiled his refusal.

'I'll drop back by later,' he said, and

continued on toward the hotel.

He had just reached the structure housing the barber shop and was abreast the passageway that lay between it and its neighbor, another small saloon, when a figure stepped out of the darkness and halted him.

'You the fellow looking for Monte Jackson?'

Royce's hand had dropped swiftly to the pistol on his hip at the unexpected interruption. Swearing deeply to vent his irritation and the tension that had shot through him, he nodded.

'That's me. Ernshaw send you?'

'Yeh,' the man answered and drew back slightly as Jake sucked hard on his cigar, flaring the coal that he might have a better look at the bar owner's messenger. He was young, narrow of face, had dark hair, and wore a red bandanna around his neck.

'Where is he?'

'Got hisself holed up in an old shack about five miles south of town. Can easy find it—got a big chinaberry tree alongside it.'

'He there alone?'

'I reckon so. Anyways, Ernshaw said you'd best go right out there—tonight if you're wanting to see him, 'cause he's leaving in the morning, early.'

CHAPTER NINETEEN

Royce grunted his understanding, looked off down the street at the hotel. He was tired, and the prospect of going up against a man with Monte Jackson's reputation was not encouraging; but if the outlaw was riding out, it would be smart to make a move now. Once gone from Kiowa Springs, Jackson could be hard to find. But the thought of a good bed at the hotel, a night's sleep—

'You for sure about him leaving?' he asked.

There was no reply. Jake came back around hastily. The man was gone. Royce grinned slightly, rubbed at his chin. Monte Jackson wielded a big stick in Kiowa Springs—that was clear. Dave Ernshaw's courier had lost no time in leaving once he had delivered his message, apparently not wanting anyone to know that he had anything to do with the matter.

Royce leaned back against the corner of the buildings housing the barber shop and puffed thoughtfully on his stogie. After a time, as his glance drifted along the deserted street, which was now lit to some extent by three or four window lamps that had come to life, but mostly by the moon and stars overhead, he drew his pistol.

As well make his move now, he concluded, absently spinning the cylinder of the weapon as he checked its chambers to assure himself that it was fully loaded. The forty-five wasn't his favorite gun—the Yarbros had taken his best gun when they'd waylaid and disarmed him—but it was a dependable weapon, and he had no fear of using it.

This decided, and ready, Jake Royce holstered the pistol and, circling the barber shop to the alley behind it, walked quickly to the Great Western's stable. He approached the structure quietly, found no sign of the hostler, and pleased with that, sought out the black and saddled and bridled him. He would as soon no one—other than Ernshaw and the messenger—knew that he had made the ride out to where Jackson was holed up. If all went well he could go there, do what he was to be paid for, and return without anyone being aware that he'd even been gone. A wry grin pulled at Jake Royce's mouth. How easily and quickly he had slipped into the ways of an outlaw!

The gelding was ready, and Royce led him out of the stable. Keeping in the shadows of the alley, he continued on foot until he was well away from the hotel and other nearby buildings. Then, pausing, he swung up into the saddle and, getting his bearings from the dipper, headed due south on a road that would lead, eventually, to Mexico.

He kept the gelding off the hard surface of the road and on the shoulder where the black's hoofs would make less noise. It was a normal, natural precaution to take, but the idea that he was thinking, again, as an outlaw would—sly and scheming—crossed his mind and set up its disturbance.

But such wasn't true, he reassured himself. He was actually going to perform a service in ridding the country of a man like Monte Jackson was said to be. Jackson was no better than any other outlaw he'd been forced to shoot down, so he should have no qualms where the man was concerned. Yet Jake Royce was finding it hard to convince himself; somehow, it was all different.

He looked ahead. He was several miles from town now, and the shack where Jackson was hiding should be near. About him the night was enchanting—soft and warm with a canopy of darkest velvet strewn with sparkling stars and a silver disc moon overhead. Far off in the shadowy short hills to the west, coyotes were in full voice as they carried on their discordant communications and in the trees that bordered the road a dove called mournfully.

He saw the shack just after making a turn in the well-defined trail. It sat a short distance back on land that evidently had once been cleared but now, through neglect and disuse, was studded with rabbitbush, Apache plume, and other rank growth. A lone tree, tall and broadly spreading, grew alongside the decaying place, extending its thickly leafed branches over the decaying structure as if to shelter it from the elements.

Royce swung off the road and halted when he came to what appeared to be the edge of the yard. Faint light was seeping from a window in the front of the shack, escaping from the sides of the blind that had been drawn. Movement in a corral not far to the right indicated the presence of a horse. Jake smiled in grim satisfaction. Monte Jackson was there.

Coming from the saddle, Royce tied the gelding to a stout bush and, avoiding the narrow path that wound its way through the clumps of brush and weeds, started for the old structure. Shortly he came to the clearing in which it stood.

The rank growth was less in evidence there, as if someone had made a half-hearted effort to keep it from overwhelming the place, and had only partly succeeded. Hunkered there, at the fringe of the yard, Royce studied the shack more closely.

There was but one horse in the corral, and such would indicate that Jackson was alone. Of course, there could be another enclosure, or possibly a barn somewhere around in back where there could be more stock—but that didn't seem likely to Jake. If Monte Jackson had company, logically, they would have put their mounts in the same corral as his.

146

The light streak still showed along the edges of the window blind, and now Jake could see the outline of the door around which light was also visible. There were no sounds coming from inside the cabin, and Royce guessed the outlaw was sleeping or perhaps doing something that required no activity.

There was only one way to handle the situation, Royce concluded; he'd simply go up to the door, kick it open, and throw himself forward into the room. He'd have his gun out and ready, and when Monte Jackson brought up his, he'd fire. Then it would be over and Riley McQueen would owe him a thousand dollars. And there was something else that incident would mark: he would have become a hired gun in the true sense of the words.

Royce rolled that about in his mind for a long minute, liked the idea even less than when it had occurred to him earlier. But again, the knowledge that Monte Jackson was an outlaw, a criminal, had its way with him, alleviating the uncomfortable feeling of guilt that persisted in plaguing him.

The country would sustain no loss with the death of Monte Jackson; in fact, the people in it would be far better off with him dead, just as it was with the death of any and all others like him. So be it. But what about the next job— the next man he could be hired by someone to kill?

Maybe he wouldn't be an outlaw; maybe it

would be just a matter of hard feelings or a grudge between two honest men. What would he do then? How could he justify in his own conscience—as a man and a hired gun—killing under those circumstances?

Royce shrugged, drew his pistol, and quietly tested the hammer. The hell with all that kind of stewing and fretting about what might happen tomorrow—or next month! He'd do the job he'd agreed to do for Riley McQueen and think about the future later.

Glancing about to be certain he was still alone in the soft, silver night, Jake, pistol in hand, started across the relatively cleared yard for the shack. He had taken no more than ten paces when the dry rasp of cloth scraping against brush brought him to a sudden halt and dropped him into a crouch.

Instantly three figures, bent low, emerged from the shadows at the sides of the shack. Warning bells clanged loud in Royce's brain, and even as the three men began to fire at him, he was going down, throwing himself full length and rolling frantically for the protection of the nearest brush.

Gaining a thick clump, curses tumbling from his lips, Jake came to his knees, gun up. His first shot sent one of the bushwhackers stumbling back. The second dropped another. And then as he flung himself again to one side, changing positions when bullets began to pluck at him, he triggered his weapon a third time.

The last of the trio, crouched and firing into the brush clump where Royce had been, stiffened, hung motionless for a long breath, and then toppled heavily to the weedy ground.

Nerves steady, the coolness that never deserted him at such critical moments still possessing him, Royce rolled to his back and sat up, as the mingled odor of dust and powder smoke reached his nostrils and filled the night air with a thin haze. He rolled out the spent cartridges in the cylinder of his pistol and reloaded.

He sat for a few moments listening, wary now and not certain that it was all over, that there were not others still lurking about seeking to kill him. And then, with that thought, realization swept through him, filling him with a soaring anger.

It was an ambush! Riley McQueen had sent him into an ambush! Why?

CHAPTER TWENTY

Grim, seething, Jake Royce drew himself to his knees and swept the moonlight-flooded yard with a quick but thorough glance. The three bushwhackers lay where they had fallen—two motionless and apparently dead, the third stirring weakly.

Royce still did not rise. There could be another man somewhere in the shadows—even more than one. Riley McQueen, having gone to so much trouble to get him killed, would not have done things halfway. He could neither hear nor see any indication of others, however. But cautious nevertheless, he gained his feet and, bent low, circled wide and came up to the house from the rear.

Two additional horses were tied to the hitch rack off to one side, and those added to the one standing Slack-hipped in the corral, probably meant that only three men participated in the ambush. Accepting that bit of logic but not relying completely upon it, Jake continued along the south side of the house to the window he noted in the wall. The shade had been drawn, as in the one in the front, but through a tear in a lower corner he was afforded a view of the shack's interior.

A table upon which sat a lamp, two broken chairs, a small cook stove with nearby shelves for provisions which were bare, a bunk against one wall, and nothing else. It was clear no one had lived there recently—and doubly certain nobody was inside at that moment.

For a long minute Royce waited quietly in the darkness close to the shack, and then, fully convinced there was no one else anywhere in the area, he moved out into the yard and crossed to the nearest figure, sprawled grotesquely in the short weeds.

Squatting, Jake took the pistol from the man's stiffening fingers and threw it off into the brush. That done, and shifting his own weapon from right hand to left, he gripped the man's face between a thumb and forefinger and turned it to the light. It was the messenger sent to him, supposedly, by Dave Ernshaw.

Jaw clamped shut, anger continuing to flow through him; Royce moved to the next lifeless shape; he followed a like procedure after getting rid of the man's weapon, which had dropped from his nerveless hand and lay close by. A stranger. Jake could not recall ever having seen him before.

He turned then to the last member of the bushwhacking party, still alive and moaning in pain. As he drew near, Royce impatiently kicked the pistol, still clutched in the man's hand, off into the weeds, and knelt beside him.

'Help me—for the love of God—help me—'

Royce seized the man by the front of his shirt, jerked him roughly about to where he

151

could see his face. A fresh spurt of curses burst from his lips. It was Ernshaw, the bartender.

'What the hell's this all about?' Jake demanded, shaking the man savagely.

'I'm shot—bad—dying,' Ernshaw mumbled. 'You got to help me.'

'Like hell I do!' Royce snapped. 'I can leave you right here with your dry-gulching friends, if I want—let the coyotes and the buzzards take care of you.'

Ernshaw struggled, tried to rise, but failed and sank back exhausted from the effort. 'No—please help—'

'Then you best start talking!' Royce shouted. 'Who hired you to kill me?'

There was no doubt in Jake's mind what the answer would be, but habits acquired in his many years as a lawman insisted that he be certain and have no doubts.

'McQueen—Riley McQueen,' Ernshaw said in a slow, laboring voice. 'You—you promising to help me?'

'I'll do what I can as long as you speak up. Why'd McQueen want me dead?'

The saloonman sighed wearily. 'I don't know. Come into my place with Jed Parker—he's one of them over there—said he had a proposition for us. Said he'd pay us five hundred dollars to—'

Ernshaw's voice broke off abruptly as a fit of coughing seized him. Royce, his motive purely selfish and in no way acting in kindness,

152

slipped an arm under the suffering man's shoulders and raised him slightly so that he might be more comfortable. The bullet had hit him, Jake saw, in the chest, and the wound was seeping blood continuously. Pulling off his bandanna, he shaped it into a pad and pressed it against the wound. There were still some questions he wanted the answer to, and only Dave Ernshaw could supply them.

'Who's this Monte Jackson?' he asked after the coughing had ceased. 'He just a name?'

'That's all—just a name,' Ernshaw replied, relieving Jake of holding the pad by taking over himself. He seemed some stronger, apparently cheered and bolstered by Royce's promise of aid. 'Was sort of a code. McQueen told us he'd send a man to my place asking for Monte Jackson. Whoever it was that done that was the man he wanted killed.'

Jake gave that thought, marveling at the well thought-out scheme that the rancher had put into action. Around them on the weedy flat, now that the disturbing sounds of violence had faded and the soft, bright night was again quiet, insects had resumed their clicking while rustlings in the dry grass here and there betrayed movements of small creatures, again abroad.

'You didn't ask him why?'

'No hope. Jed Parker was the one that made the deal with McQueen. Jed's kind of a drifter—comes and goes. Usually hangs

153

around town when there ain't no cattle drives going on.'

'Who's your other partner?'

Ernshaw stirred, coughed again. 'I'm kind of petering out. Ain't you about done asking me things?'

'Not till I get it all straight,' Royce said. 'Who's your other partner?'

'Name's Pete Sutton. We rung him in on it 'cause McQueen said he wanted the job done right and figured it'd take three men shooting to do it. Said you'd be hard to kill.' Ernshaw paused, brushed at his eyes with his free hand. 'He sure was right.'

'And you're for sure you don't know why McQueen went to all this trouble?'

'Nope, before God I don't. Like I told you, it was Parker that made the deal. Could be McQueen told him, but he sure never told Sutton or me. You going to get me to town like you promised?'

Royce, struggling to puzzle out a reason for the rancher's wanting him dead, sifted through his memory searching for the name McQueen and for something that would explain the man's hatred. He could come up with nothing, failed even to recall ever having heard the rancher's name before that day in Parsonville when he presented himself at the marshal's office.

'You hearing me, Mister? You going to help—'

'You don't even know my name, do you,' Royce broke in shrugging. 'You were going to kill me, but you don't know who I am or what I do.'

Ernshaw again brushed at his eyes as if seeking to displace some hindrance to vision, and moved his head slowly from side to side.

'No, can't say as I do. Maybe McQueen told me, but I don't recollect. All I know was that when a man showed up looking for Monte Jackson, he was the one Jed and Pete and me was to take care of . . . They both dead—Pete and Jed?'

Royce nodded. 'McQueen already pay you?'

'Nope. Jed was to do the collecting after we was done. Was to take along something to prove you was dead— papers you'd be carrying, maybe.'

'Where was he to meet McQueen?'

'At his ranch—the Q Bar.'

'Where is it from here?'

'East—maybe twenty-five miles or so.'

Royce smiled tightly. Riley McQueen was due to have a visitor all right, but not the one he was expecting, and one who was going to demand a lot of answers—and who just might be the last visitor he'd ever see!

'How do I find the place?'

'Head east out of town. Road runs right to McQueen's.' Ernshaw paused, went into another coughing spasm. When it was over, he looked up at Royce, gripped his arm. 'You

155

ain't going off an leaving me here, are you, Mister? I—I sure don't want to lay here and die—let them lousy coyotes and stinking buzzards fight over me. I'm begging you, mister, please—'

'Which one's your horse?' Royce asked, rising. 'One in the corral or one of those out back?'

'The buckskin—out back. I'll sure be grateful to you if you—'

Jake Royce was already moving off toward the rear of the shack where the two horses were tethered. He'd stand by his promise and do what he could for Dave Ernshaw, although he owed the man absolutely nothing—and then light out for McQueen's Q Bar ranch.

Coming to the horses, he released them and led them back to where Ernshaw and his partners lay, pausing long enough enroute to collect the third mount frond the corral as he did.

Loading the dead men across the saddles of their animals, and tying them securely so they would not slide off, Royce then helped the saloon keeper onto his buckskin. He jammed his feet into the stirrups and wound the reins about his hands to prevent the man from losing control of his horse and falling off.

That done, he linked all three animals together with a rope he found on one of the saddles, and with Ernshaw's buckskin in the lead, he returned to where he'd left the black gelding.

'You—you just leaving me here?' Ernshaw asked as Royce released his grip on the buckskin's bridle after pointing him toward the road to Kiowa Springs.

'Far as I go,' Jake said, swinging up onto the saddle.

'But I ain't sure I can—'

'Your problem,' Royce said bluntly. He was not forgetting that Ernshaw and his two friends had done their best to kill him only minutes earlier. 'Hang onto the horn with one hand and the lines with the other, and head out. Your horse'll do the rest.'

Ernshaw shook his head. 'But I can't do that! I got to hold that rag against the bullet hole—'

'You can manage,' Jake said coldly, and added: 'When you get to town, be damn sure you tell the straight of what happened out here. Do a lot of lying and I'll look you up when I come back through, and—'

'Don't worry—I won't do no lying!' Ernshaw declared anxiously. 'I'll tell just how it was, how you—'

But Jake Royce heard only the first few words. He was already cutting across the flat, heading east for the McQueen ranch.

CHAPTER TWENTY-ONE

On a low bluff overlooking a broad, grassy swale, Jake Royce pulled his horse to a stop. Below, clearly visible in the rising dawn, lay McQueen's Q Bar ranch.

The anger that had swept through the tall, ex-lawman at the time he had discovered the rancher's deception had dissipated but little, and now as he looked down upon the McQueen holdings, it became even more intense. Riley McQueen would pay in full for the double cross he had pulled—regardless of his reason for doing so. He had accepted the proposition the rancher had made in good faith, and only the lowest kind of man would take advantage of another's trust and send him into an ambush.

The ranch was stirring life. Lamplight was now showing in the bunkhouse as well as the cookshack, which stood off to one side of a larger, elongated building—undoubtedly the dining quarters. No sign of anyone awakening had yet appeared, however, in the main house, which was built forward and considerably apart from the other structures; and Royce had the unsettling thought that McQueen might not be there, was instead away for some reason.

He speculated on that for a time, shaping a

plan in his mind as to what he would do if such proved true. Meanwhile he idly watched the cowhands appear and sleepily head for the long building where they would have their morning meal. Two other members of the Q Bar crew bringing up horses from somewhere behind the large barn, hazing them along a narrow alleyway between that structure and the bunkhouse and turning them into one of the several corrals.

At that moment the front door of the main house opened. Royce swore quietly in relief as the screen swung back and Riley McQueen, yawning and stretching, walked out onto the porch and, halting at its edge, stared off into the east at the streaks of color brightening the sky.

'Take a good look, damn you!' Royce muttered, his voice taut with anger. 'It's going to be the last time you see the sun come up.'

McQueen remained on the porch for several minutes, enjoying his view and the crisp, fresh air. Then he turned, walked off the porch, circled the house, and made his way to the crew's dining room.

Royce nodded grimly in satisfaction. McQueen ate with his cowhands; that was near-positive proof that he lived alone and that he had no cook or other help working in the ranchhouse.

Stirring, finally taking note of the effects of the long, hard ride he'd just made, Jake came off his saddle and, feet planted solidly on the ground, flexed his arms and legs, relieving as much as he could the stiffness that gripped his muscles.

There was nothing he could do for the time being, but he had learned what he needed to know; McQueen was there and would be alone in the house—not that the latter made any great difference. Any man interfering or getting in the way would be asking for trouble.

Hunched now on his heels, the black nuzzling at the thin grass growing on the crest of the brush bluff, Jake continued to study the scatter of buildings in the swale. All were in fine condition and reflected continual upkeep. A rail fence, the poles neatly whitewashed, surrounded the yard encircling the main house, separating it from the working part of the ranch, and a high gate with a square-hewed crosspiece from which hung the sign, Q BAR RANCH RILEY MCQUEEN & SON, OWNERS, marked the entrance to the premises.

McQueen's range evidently ran to the south and west in fairly level, grass-covered land. Trees could be seen here and there offering shade from the Texas sun to the grazing cattle, and a windmill with a large pond near its base provided water for the cows as well as for the house.

There was a stream visible, too, a narrow ribbon, sparkling in the growing light as it

160

twisted southward across the flats and between the low, bubblelike hills. Viewing it all thoughtfully, Royce pulled off his hat and rubbed at the back of his head, still a bit tender—thanks to the Yarbros. Why would a man like McQueen, with a fine, successful ranch such as the Q Bar, stoop to murder? If ever a man ought—

Jake drew himself upright slowly. The cowhands, breakfast over, were coming from the dining hall, some of them heading for the bunkhouse to get the gear they would need, while others, already equipped, were angling for the corral where they would rope out the horse they would ride that day. Riley McQueen should be putting in his appearance, too.

Royce, motionless behind a stand of wild berry bushes, watched the men saddle up and begin to move out, a few having to master wildly pitching horses, spirited in the early morning coolness, before they could get themselves set.

While they were moving off, McQueen came through the doorway of the dining hall, strolled out into the yard, and halted near the corral. Two riders veered their mounts about and trotted up to him. The three held a brief conversation, ending it when the punchers spurred off to join the rest of the crew and McQueen sauntered slowly back to the main house.

Jake watched the rancher enter, saw him close the screen but prop open the wooden door so that the morning coolness might enter and fill the structure and perhaps hold off the day's heat for a time.

Royce, pulling down his hat, mounted the black and, cutting wide to get off the bluff, approached the house from its lower side. He took no particular care to remain unseen since there was no blind wall in the structure—there were windows on all sides—and while there was considerable scrubby growth outside the rail fence, the yard immediately surrounding the house was covered with short grass.

Deadly calm, Royce reached the wide gate, turned in, and rode directly to the hitch rack placed a few paces to the left of the porch. Halting there, he left the saddle, wrapped the black's reins around the crossbar, and hefting the pistol on his hip—a long-observed precautionary habit designed to assure him that the weapon was free and unencumbered in its holster—stepped up onto the porch.

Crossing to the door, he pulled it open. Letting himself into the house, he found he was in the parlor—a square room in which there were several leather chairs, a library table with a film of dust on its surface along with a copy of the Bible and a yellowing newspaper. A flowered rug covered the floor, and there were framed pictures, probably of relatives, on the walls.

Royce, taut, hesitated in the center of the room to listen. A hallway led off its back corner, and from somewhere along its length the sound of rustling paper reached Jake. McQueen evidently had an office farther down and was at that moment working in it.

Taking matches from his shirt pocket, Royce wedged them into his spurs, locking them into silence, and then—gun in hand, jaw set, his customarily narrowed eyes now shut down to little more than angry, burning slits— he moved into the hallway.

Carpeting also covered the floor of the narrow corridor, and with spurs muted, he was able to proceed silently, passing first a bedroom on his right, another to his left, and then a small alcove with shelves on the walls that served as a storage area.

Ahead almost at the end of the hall, was a doorway. Opposite it a second opening led into what was probably a kitchen and dining room used by the McQueen family when at home. Royce gave that thought; from the sign above the gate, there was, or once had been a family. Where were they now?

But that was of no interest to Jake Royce as he looked ahead. The room to his left at the end of the corridor could only be the one where the rancher was. Tense, Royce continued. He was certain there was no one else in the house, but upon reaching the door to the office, he halted to listen. There were sounds coming from the yard where some of the hired help, probably the cook and his swamper, or perhaps the stable hands, were going about chores of one kind or another.

Certain now that all was in his favor, Royce stepped suddenly and silently into the room at the end of the hall. He had been right—it was the rancher's office. Riley McQueen was sitting at a rolltop desk, a pencil in hand, a sheaf of papers before him. The area was small, barren, with a solitary calendar advertising whiskey on one wall, the picture of a grave-faced woman on another. A rifle stood propped in one corner while a belted pistol hung from the back of the chair he was using.

A hard, humorless smile cracked Royce's mouth. 'Howdy, McQueen,' he said.

CHAPTER TWENTY-TWO

Riley McQueen whirled in his chair. His mouth dropped open, and his eyes flared in shock and surprise.

'My God—Royce! I—' he blurted, stumbling over the words.

Jake smiled crookedly. 'Figured I'd be dead by now, that it, McQueen? Or maybe I'm a ghost come to square the score with you.'

The rancher's eyes were still filled with fear, and a whiteness was now showing at the corners of his jaw. 'I—I wasn't expecting to see—'

'Can bet you wasn't,' Royce said coldly. 'Now, back up there against the wall. I want you looking at me when I put a bullet into your heart.'

McQueen, moving slowly, rose to his feet and sidled to the place Royce was indicating with a pointing finger.

'You—you can't just shoot me down—'

'The hell I can't!' Jake snapped angrily, kicking the door shut behind him. 'It'll be just as easy as it was for you to hire them three jaspers to bushwhack me!'

Riley McQueen passed a trembling hand over his mouth, brushing at it nervously. Although it was cool in the room, sweat was standing out on his forehead in large beads.

'You ain't—won't get away with this,' he said, stammering. 'There's men out there in the yard. They'll hear the shot, come to see what—'

'They won't ever notice it,' Royce cut in. 'Not when I jam the muzzle of my gun into your middle and pull the trigger. Shot'll be muffled. But before I do that, I want to know one thing, McQueen—why'd you set me up for killing? I never saw you before in my life.'

The rancher released a long, ragged breath, swiped at the sweat on his face. 'You murdered my boy—that's why!' he shouted in a cracked voice. 'Murdered him—killed my wife—ruined everything for me!'

Jake Royce frowned, stared. 'Your son? I don't recollect ever—'

'Of course you don't! That's the kind of a man you are—a cold-blooded killer who never knows who he's murdering—and never cares! They ain't people—they ain't even names to you—they're just something you put a bullet into and blow away their lives!'

Royce's eyes appeared closed as he studied the rancher, and there was a tautness to the weather-browned skin of his face.

'Done what I had to when I was doing my job. And I never wasted much time thinking about the outlaws I was sent to bring in.'

'Bring in!' McQueen echoed distractedly. 'You never took the trouble to bring my boy in! You just shot him down cold—a kid—just turned eighteen.'

'Eighteen's plenty old enough to know the difference between right and wrong,' Jake said. 'And there has to be more to it than you're telling. When was this—and where?'

'Down near Fort Worth—town they called Haleyville. Was three years ago, about. Dan was with a couple of friends. They were just having themselves a big time, celebrating, sowing wild oats that's all it was. Then they got into devilment of some kind, and you and a deputy sheriff went after them.'

Royce was still frowning, but the anger had faded from him, and a vague sort of guilt was filtering in, replacing it. He had suddenly realized that most of the men he had been forced to kill were nameless in his mind, and that fact, now heavy on his conscience, was disturbing and shaming him.

'You don't remember the time at all do you?' McQueen pressed. 'It wasn't nothing to you a'tall!'

'Got to admit I don't recollect—'

'You was there on business. The deputy figured he needed help and asked you to back him up. Was told that later—and it took me all this time to find you. You remembering now?'

'Maybe. Sounds to me like your boy was mixed up in something a lot worse than you claim, else the law there wouldn't've gone after him. What about the deputy?'

'He got himself killed before I could do

anything about him. Another reason why it took so long to run you down. He was dead, and there wasn't nobody knew who you were or where you were from till I got the sheriff to look into the court records and figure out who it was that was passing through about that time. Was you—and you was delivering a prisoner to the Fort Worth marshal.'

Royce shrugged, listened briefly to sounds in the yard. 'Said it before—was doing my job—'

'Job—hell! You didn't have to kill my Danny! Folks said you just opened up on them boys with your guns, that you didn't give them a chance!'

Again a strange feeling of guilt stirred through Jake Royce. He still couldn't recall the incident—but why should he? He'd delivered dozens of prisoners to different towns over the years and taking one to Fort Worth couldn't have possibly made an impression on him. Yet—if there had been a shootout—killing—

'Boy of yours had to be asking for trouble,' he said, impatiently brushing aside the growing thread of doubt. 'Was likely shooting at the deputy and me. 'I've never yet gunned down a man unless he was coming at me. I—'

There was an abrupt pounding on the door. A voice shouted, 'Mr. McQueen?'

Royce pulled to one side, moved his leveled pistol warningly at the rancher. 'Watch

168

yourself,' he said softly.

'Mr. McQueen—you in there?' the voice called again.

The door opened a few inches. A man, one of the yard hands, judging from the overalls and thick-soled shoes he wore, thrust himself partly into the room. He caught sight of McQueen standing back against the wall, and then of Royce facing the rancher from across the room—the pistol on his hand lowered and not visible.

'Sure didn't know you had company, Mr. McQueen,' the man said, apologetically. 'You want me to come back later?'

The rancher glanced at Jake, looked away. 'No, it's all right, Harry. What's the trouble?'

'Well, that there breeding bull you bought's got out again. Busted down the corral. Was wondering if you wanted us to go rope him and bring him back, or leave him run loose for a spell.'

'Let him run,' McQueen said indifferently, and then, as Harry started to withdraw into the hallway, made as if to say more. A shake of the head from Royce, however, stilled the words he intended to say before they could be voiced.

Harry pulled the door closed carefully, and for a few moments the thump of his heavy shoes could be heard on the floor of the adjoining kitchen as he crossed it on his way to the yard.

McQueen had regained his composure

169

somewhat and now considered Royce with a scornful smile. 'You would have killed me if I'd said something you didn't like to Harry, wouldn't you?'

Royce nodded. 'Can bet on it—and saying something wrong to him could've got him killed, too. I would've had to stop him.'

The rancher's eyes flamed. 'You see! Killing don't mean a damn thing to you! Hell—you're not a man, you're not something human—you can kill easy as another man can take a breath.

'Royce, you're a dead thing yourself—as cold and lifeless as that pistol you live by, with no more feeling in your heart or blood in your veins than a chunk of steel!'

Jake, pistol again up and leveled at the rancher, smiled grimly. 'Go ahead—shoot off your mouth, say what you want. But if you're trying to talk me out of killing you, you're wasting your breath. No man sets me up and gets away with it.'

'I'd figure on you saying that—and it's too damn bad Parker and them bungled the job I hired them to do. The country'd be a lot better off without you—your kind.'

Doubt once again moved into Jake Royce's thoughts, clouding his mind. He'd used those same words himself to justify the shooting of some wanted outlaw—now it was being applied to him. And he was being called bloodless, as lifeless as the pistol he carried—and Riley McQueen meant every hate-laden

170

word he uttered.

It was nothing new. Royce had heard them all before and seen the livid loathing in the eyes of those who had spoken them. He was despised, considered a monster with neither heart nor soul. Time was when he had paid no mind to such, believed it to be a part of being a good lawman—but now the words were going deep and were the source of the doubt that had risen within him.

He had been truthful in telling McQueen that he did not remember shooting his son—and that fact was suddenly haunting him. *He should remember!* He should recall the face and name of every man he'd shot down, every life he'd taken. Why couldn't he? Was it some kind of inner defense that, to protect him from his conscience, wiped all detail of such from his mind?

If so, then it was true that he was a cold-blooded monster, a heartless killer using his weapon without remorse while lulling himself into the belief that it was all being done for the sake of law. Was that really the way of it? Had he, through all the years of wearing a star, blinded himself to the truth?

'You came here to kill me,' Royce heard McQueen say. 'Well, damn you to hell—go right ahead. I stopped living when you murdered my boy. The same goes for my wife. When you killed Danny, you might as well have come and put a bullet in her because she

171

never got over his death—just pined away and died.

'That's one more reason why I wanted you dead and why I don't give a damn about what happens to me. I've been living for the day when I got you killed, and then I figured I could quit—quit everything. Already put my ranch up for sale so you can see I'm telling you straight.

'Now, go right ahead, Royce—do what you come here to do. I heard somebody say back there in Parsonville that you wasn't a man no more, that instead you was just a gun—and that's pure gospel if ever I heard any. Now, I'll even get my pistol there and be holding it in my hand so's you can tell folks it was self-defense when you killed me. That way you won't spoil your record none.

'But there's one thing I'd like to know, Royce. What number will I be? Will I be the fifteenth man you've murdered? Or maybe I'll be the twentieth—or thirtieth. Which one, Royce—or like the names of them you've killed, maybe can't you remember that either?'

Jake Royce stood quiet, eyes on the floor. He shook his head. Suddenly what he intended to do to McQueen no longer was important or necessary. He looked at the pistol in his hand, and the thought came to him that with it it was easy to kill, to take a life; without it, a man could go in peace and, perhaps, without hate— and, he realized suddenly, he'd had enough of hate and death.

'Forget it, McQueen,' he said, slipping his weapon back into its holster. 'I'm letting it end here.'

CHAPTER TWENTY-THREE

Riley McQueen's rigid shape relented slightly. He stared at Royce unbelievingly. 'You saying you're not going to use your gun on me?'

Jake shrugged. 'You heard right. I've holstered it—maybe for good.'

The rancher seemed not to understand the change that had come over Royce. 'That mean you're leaving here, letting things go— forgetting what I tried to do?'

'That's the size of it. I've been packing a gun long enough, and maybe there's been times when I was a mite too quick to use it—but I'm done with that now. I'm heading back home— my real home, Ohio. Woman there that once meant a lot to me, and me to her. Once said if I ever changed my way of living to look her up, that she'd be waiting. It's been awhile—but maybe she still is.'

Royce turned slowly, moved toward the door. He would have to return to Kiowa Springs and collect his belongings, left in the room he'd rented at the hotel. He could sell his horse and saddle there, too, and then catch the train he'd heard whistling the night before. Likely there was a stagecoach in the settlement that conveyed passengers to it.

Reaching the door, Jake paused, the old caution again taking charge. Laying his shuttered glance on the rancher, now standing by his desk, he considered the man coldly.

'I said it ended here. That goes for your side of it, too. That clear?'

McQueen, silent, only stared.

'You've got no reason to kill me—and you know it. And it's not as good as the one I have to gun you down. I'm passing mine up. You do the same and we'll call it even.'

'Whatever you say,' the rancher murmured.

Royce opened the door, started to pass through it into the hallway. He hesitated, looked back at McQueen. 'Want to say I'm sorry about your wife, and your boy, too. Like for you to know that.'

'Sure, sure,' the rancher replied as Jake stepped out into the corridor and pulled the door closed behind him.

Turning, he headed back up the carpeted hallway for the front of the house. It wouldn't be hard to hang up his guns, he assured himself. He'd spent a lot of days in the saddle, under all kinds of conditions—cold, heat, wind, snow, and rain—had hung around every conceivable sort of town, all in the interest of upholding the law.

Now it would be good to go back east, settle down where such things were unknown— where he'd never have to use a gun again and there'd be no need to walk quietly in the dark or keep an eye over a shoulder—

Alarm rocked through Jake Royce. The dry

rustle of cloth in the hallway behind him had come to his ears. Someone was slipping up on him. Instantly Jake whirled—drew—fired. In that same fraction of time, he saw the taut, hating features of Riley McQueen, saw also the leveled pistol in his hand. He should have known; a hate such as the rancher had for him could never die.

Royce felt the brush of McQueen's bullet, triggered hastily, as it cut across his arm. He had pressed off his shot hurriedly, too, taking no time to aim but relying on instinct and experience to direct his accuracy. As the room echoed with the thunder of the dual explosions and smoke belched into swirling clouds within its walls, Jake saw the rancher stagger against one of the chairs and sink to the floor.

Cursing, Royce crossed quickly to the man and wrenched the pistol from his hand. Throwing it into a far corner of the parlor, he squatted beside the rancher.

'What the hell's the matter with you?' he demanded hotly, pulling McQueen's shirt aside to examine the wound made by his bullet. It was high in the chest area, had missed vital organs and passed cleanly through the rancher's body.

'You'll live,' Royce said bluntly, coming up right. Turning his head, he spent a few moments listening. He doubted the gunshots would have been heard by the men in the yard, but he was taking nothing for granted. He could hear no sounds of anyone approaching.

'I reckon this changes things,' he said, bringing his attention back to McQueen. 'Now, you've got me figured for a killer—nothing more than a gun, you said. Seeing how you feel, I think I'd be smart to go ahead, prove you're right, and put another bullet into you where it'd do the most good.'

The rancher had pulled himself to a sitting position, and now, shoulders to the wall and pressing a handkerchief to his wound, he returned Royce's glance coldly.

'Go ahead, damn you,' he muttered. 'Go on, shoot me again. It's what I'm expecting you to do.'

Royce considered the man dispassionately for a long breath, and then holstering his pistol, shook his head.

'The hell with it,' he said, and pivoting, passed through the doorway out onto the porch.

Crossing the landing, Jake walked to where the black was tied and, freeing the lines, swung up onto the saddle. McQueen would never forget—or forgive—he realized, as he rode out of the yard.

'Marshal—pull up!'

At the sharp call, coming from a stand of brush just beyond the tall gate, Royce drew the gelding to a halt. The voice was familiar, but in that moment he could not place it.

'What's this all about?' he asked, letting his hand sink slowly toward the pistol at his side.

'Don't try it, Marshal,' the voice warned. 'Raise your arms and turn around.'

In the quiet of the morning broken by the distant cawing of crows and the clink of hammering back in McQueen's barn, Jake kneed the black slowly about. A wry grin pulled down his lips . . . Dallas Yarbro.

'Figured I'd lost you,' he said.

Yarbro, pistol leveled, wagged his head. 'Sort of done that back there on the road, but when I seen after a spell that you wasn't ahead of me, I doubled back and took that side road to that town Yankee. Found out you'd been there and gone to a place called Kiowa Springs.

'Got there and first thing I learned was how you killed off two fellows and shot up another'n so's he's sure to die. I done a mite of talking to him, and he said you was coming here to this ranch. Rode right out and've been waiting ever since.'

'You come close to getting here too late—'

Dallas nodded. 'Scared me some thinking maybe somebody'd beat me to killing you, but like always, you come through with a whole hide . . . But you ain't this time.'

Royce shrugged, looked off across the grassy flats of McQueen range. He wasn't fnished with his way of life, after all. Dallas Yarbro had to be settled with. After that was done, he could proceed with his plans to hang up his guns and go to Ohio—if he still wished.

'You sure you want this?' he asked, sighing

as he looked down at the man.

'You're damn right!' Dallas snapped. 'You figure I'd follow you all the way to here if I didn't? It's what I come for.'

'All right—it's your party. Put your gun away while I climb down, and we'll start from scratch.'

A sneer crossed Yarbro's face. 'Go ahead, climb down—but I ain't putting my gun away. I ain't that dumb!'

Royce smiled. 'You want me to draw while you're standing there with your pistol pointed at me—that it?'

'Just how it's going to be,' Yarbro replied. 'I'm giving you the same chance as you probably gave my sister.'

'Wrong again!' Jake shouted and dug his spurs into the gelding's flanks. As the big horse lunged toward Yarbro, he drew his pistol and fired.

Dallas triggered his weapon in that same fragment of time, but the sudden, unexpected charge of the gelding destroyed his aim. Royce flinched as the bullet whipped at the sleeve of his shirt. Yarbro, much less fortunate, took the full impact of Jake's forty-five slug in the heart.

As the smoke and dust cleared, Royce looked down at the lifeless body of Dallas Yarbro. Back at McQueen's, two men, attracted by the gunshots, were standing in the yard behind the house watching, apparently still unaware that the Q Bar's owner was inside with a bullet wound. Ignoring them, Jake continued to stare at Yarbro. *How many dead men does this make?* he seemed to hear a voice asking. *How many?*

He didn't know—and suddenly didn't care. It was the same old story, a shootout forced upon him and he came out the winner through sheer proficiency. Why should he feel guilty? Why should he be ashamed?

It was all part of being what some called a dedicated lawman—that ability and courage to use his gun when necessary regardless of the critics who never could understand that he had not killed by choice but by circumstance.

Why should he give it up? Why should he put aside the tools of the trade he knew so well and return to a humdrum life in a faraway city where he could never be really happy and would eventually die of boredom?

The hell with it—he'd not do it. He'd wrap Dallas Yarbro's body up in his blanket, load him across his saddle, and take him home to his ma and brothers. That could be a chancy proposition if they chose not to listen to his explanation, but he reckoned he could handle it.

And then he'd ride west for Arizona or maybe California. Somewhere out there he'd find a town that needed a good lawman—one not afraid to do his job.